GEEK!

High School Edition

Crystal Skillman

A SAMUEL FRENCH ACTING EDITION

SAMUEL FRENCH

FOUNDED 1830

SAMUELFRENCH.COM
SAMUELFRENCH-LONDON.CO.UK

ISBN 978-0-573-70320-1

www.SamuelFrench.com
www.SamuelFrench-London.co.uk

FOR PRODUCTION ENQUIRIES

UNITED STATES AND CANADA
Info@SamuelFrench.com
1-866-598-8449

UNITED KINGDOM AND EUROPE
Plays@SamuelFrench-London.co.uk
020-7255-4302

Each title is subject to availability from Samuel French, depending upon country of performance. Please be aware that *GEEK! HIGH SCHOOL EDITION* may not be licensed by Samuel French in your territory. Professional and amateur producers should contact the nearest Samuel French office or licensing partner to verify availability.

MUSIC USE NOTE

Licensees are solely responsible for obtaining formal written permission from copyright owners to use copyrighted music in the performance of this play and are strongly cautioned to do so. If no such permission is obtained by the licensee, then the licensee must use only original music that the licensee owns and controls. Licensees are solely responsible and liable for all music clearances and shall indemnify the copyright owners of the play(s) and their licensing agent, Samuel French, against any costs, expenses, losses and liabilities arising from the use of music by licensees. Please contact the appropriate music licensing authority in your territory for the rights to any incidental music.

IMPORTANT BILLING AND CREDIT REQUIREMENTS

If you have obtained performance rights to this title, please refer to your licensing agreement for important billing and credit requirements.

GEEK! was first produced by the Vampire Cowboys Theatre Company at Incubator Arts Projects in New York City on March 21, 2013. The performance was directed by Robert Ross Parker, with sets and lights by Nick Francone, costumes by Kristina Makowski and Jessica Wegener Shay, sound by Shane Rettig, multimedia design by Matthew Tennie, puppet design by David Valentine, and fight direction by Ray Rodriguez. Stage management was by Kelly Ruth Cole and Shannon Lippert, and assistant stage management was by Lauren Elizabeth Erwin. The cast was as follows:

DANYA. . . . . Allison Buck

HONEY . . . . Becky Byers

TOBY/ENSEMBLE . . . . .Sheldon Best

GWEN/ENSEMBLE . . . . Emily Williams

GUARD 1/ MINNIE/SPRING/ENSEMBLE . . . . Rebecca Comtois

GUARD 2/SQUEAKER/MANNO/ENSEMBLE . . . . Eugene Oh

The producing staff of the Vampire Cowboys Theatre Company was as follows:

CO-ARTISTIC DIRECTORS. . . . . Qui Nguyen, Robert Ross Parker

PRODUCER/MANAGING DIRECTOR . . . . .Abby Marcus

PRODUCING DIRECTOR. . . . . Nick Francone

ASSOCIATE PRODUCER. . . . . Dan Rech

CHARACTERS

DANYA – Japanese-American girl, 16. Cosplays as **DANTE**, the hero of *Dante's Fire*.

HONEY – Danya's friend, 13. Cosplays as **VIRGIE**, Dante's guide.

An ensemble cast of four actors play the following roles.

Ensemble Actor 1 (female):

ELLEN – Honey's sister and Danya's best friend (pre-recorded). She cosplays as **CLEO**, the villain.

MISS COSY – Cute anime character that is an interactive guide. Miss Cosy operates as a guide/announcer for the convention. Danya and Honey utilize her throughout the play. (Miss Cosy can be a projected anime, a voiceover, a puppet, or an actor if roles are not double cast.)

MARCY – Preteen playing a *Dante's Fire* **DEVIL ANGEL**.

GWEN – Danya's arch rival from her preteen days, cosplaying as **CLEO**, the villain of *Dante's Fire*. Gwen is played by same actress who plays Ellen.

CLEO (FIGURE) – Gwen in disguise.

DEVIL CAT #1 – Woman, mid-30s, playing an evil cat lady.

GOTH GIRL PRINCESS – Bitchy yet lovely goth girl, in a Tiara, playing a princess from *Dante's Fire*.

Ensemble Actor 2 (male):

GUARD #1 – Old-timer geek, 30s. A guy into *Star Trek*.

STEAMPUNK LEUT #1 – Teen acting as Army in *Dante's Fire*.

BRIAN – Fifth grader dressed as the **TIMEKEEPER**.

GOTH BOY PRINCESS – Goth boy, dressed as princess from *Dante's Fire*.

SQUEAKER* – A guy cosplaying as the big furry orange ball-like creature.

MANNO – Kid who plays a "Wizard Magic" card game nerd.

Ensemble Actor 3 (female):

GUARD #2 – Old-timer geek, 30s. A woman into *Star Wars*.

MOLLY – Preteen playing a *Dante's Fire* **DEVIL ANGEL**.

STEAMPUNK LEUT #2 – Teen acting as Army in *Dante's Fire*.

MINNIE – Overly dramatic girl dressed as the **MINOTAUR**.

DEVIL CAT # 2 – Woman, mid-30s, playing an evil cat lady.

SPRING – Determined homeschooled larping girl who plays a French elf archer.

---

* If keeping the cast size to six actors, Squeaker may be played by different ensemble actors because he is always in a costume.

Ensemble Actor 4 (male):

TOBY – Dressed as Steampunk Army leader, **ULEE-O**. Gwen's ex-boyfriend.

BATTLE BOT BOY – Headgear-wearing third grader playing an evil robot.

TINY AJAX – Kid cosplaying a dwarf. Love to rock and roll… dice!

SETTING

An anime convention in Columbus, Ohio.

TIME

January of the present year.

PRODUCTION INFO

GEEK! High School Edition can be performed without an intermission.

DOUBLE CASTING

GEEK! High School Edition can work with or without double casting the roles. The New York premiere production was done with a cast of six: four females and two males.

Danya and Honey were always played by the same two actresses. (The actress playing Honey can play an extra background character in the elevator in Act Two, Scene 1.)

SET DESIGN

There are quick scene changes that require alternating between reality and a heightened fantasy. The set design for the New York premiere production was kept simple to allow for these fast costume and lighting changes. Several large moveable screens operated as the set and were moved about and projected on. A screen that dropped from the ceiling was used to project the girls homemade cosplay videos. Some props and set elements (like what the girls see in the museum) were simply acted out as the girls see them or acted out in the wings (like the red door).

Ultimately, the set should be adaptable and able to move quickly to keep the brisk pace of the show. There are many low budget solutions to *GEEK! High School Edition* which is, after all, a play about imagination. So have fun imagining how this play comes to life on the stage!

VIDEOS

The videos throughout the play are integral to telling the story. They reveal why the girls are there that day and are the only times we see Ellen's character. They are each scripted and will fill time during the many quick transitions needed in the play. If utilizing double casting, one will find this to be very useful.

The videos feature Danya, Honey, and Ellen cosplaying. Danya cosplays as Dante, the young male hero – tough but vulnerable. Dante's look should be strong while still embracing Danya as a girl. Honey plays Virgie, Dante's best friend and right hand gal, and her pet is Squeaker. Ellen plays Cleo, Dante's best friend turned villain.

Though most videos will be pre-recorded, the video of Danya racing through the convention and the advertisement (videos 2 and 5) can be live.

AUTHOR'S NOTES

If you've picked up this script, it's likely you're already familiar with the concept of cosplay, you smart cookie, you! But in case you're looking for a bit more information about it: cosplay is simply when you love a character in a show or comic so much, that you gather with other loyal fans – often at conventions – dressed up as that character.

In *GEEK! High School Edition* each character is cosplaying characters they love from their favorite anime/manga, *Dante's Fire,* a fictional show created for the play. In the New York premiere production, much joy came from fleshing out the character of each kid – being true to who they are as they attempt to be a larger than life character, always keeping in mind the real kid underneath. There are heightened moments in the play where each kid 'sees' themselves doing heroic acts like their characters, but in reality these are real teenagers with real problems. Being true to that is the key to the play and to the fun!

For this *High School Edition,* I'd like to give special thanks to Erin Underwood, the editor of Geek Theatre Anthology, Underwoods Press, 2014.

For more information about the origins of *GEEK! High School Edition,* read Crystal Skillman's interview at HOWLROUND.COM

FOREWORD

Whaddup reader,

First and foremost, I'm a fan of Crystal Skillman. I've watched her tear
it up in the downtown scene for years. Her voice is irreverent, but yet
also incredibly moving. What amazes me about her talents is she has
the ability to find the humanity in even the quirkiest of characters and
makes her audience absolutely fall in love with them.

With that in mind, in ye olde 2009, I invited her to write for our monthly
serialized play series, *The Saturday Night Saloon*, which has a rogues
gallery of powerhouse playwrights writing in "geek" such as Mac Rogers,
A. Rey Pamatmat, Megan Mostyn-Brown, and Mike Lew to name a few.
Ask anyone who's done it, writing six interconnected plays that has to be
both interesting as a full season arch but also immediately entertaining
as individual episodes for a packed crowd of drunken geeks is no easy
task. However Crystal blew it up.

For two seasons, she crafted two shows, *Hack* and *Killer High* (the former
being a spaghetti-western set in an office and the latter being about a
group of elementary school assassins), that both became instantaneous
audience favorites. Our rabid fans were foaming at the mouth for
Crystal's work. They sent emails. They talked to me in the streets and at
the after parties about them. They fell in love with her writing. Seeing
her mastery over our audience inspired me to commission her to write
the first Vampire Cowboys show not penned by me.

As the company known as the pioneers of "geek theatre," Vampire
Cowboys has always created shows *for* outsiders, crafting plays about
zombies and superheroes and epic space operas. However Crystal took a
different approach as I handed her the reigns, instead of creating a play
for them, she wrote a play *about* them. *GEEK!* is a love letter to all our
fellow pop-culture nerds, fangurls, and gamer-boys. It explores both the
positive and negative connotation to a word that has earned Hollywood
billions of dollars yet still isolates those who are most devoted to those
entertainments to sit alone in cafeterias. Along with all the hysterical
jokes, funny characters, and adventure, *GEEK!* is a show about the heart
of being an outsider and I am so proud that it is now available for you to
read and hopefully produce in your own communities.

I'm a fan of Crystal Skillman, but she's also one of my best friends. I am
delighted that this play is now in your hands to enjoy. Get ready to laugh.
And cry. And geek. Using a bit of Crystal Skillman's patented slang, it is
"amazeballs!"

Sincerely,
Qui Nguyen
Playwright & Co-Artistic Director, *Vampire Cowboys*

To my husband Fred,
and to all those who love creating a world to live in
where anything is possible, if you imagine it.

PRESHOW (OPTIONAL)

If desired, you can set up a convention feel in the performance space as soon as the audience enters. During preshow, projected slides of Miss Cosy, a cute little anime character, can teach audience members the rules of the anime convention they are about to see. These slides will introduce the audience to the fun world of *Dante's Fire!*

Welcome to Dante's Fire Con! Miss Cosy's Dos & Don'ts!

SLIDE #1: WELCOME TO DANTE'S FIRE CON! Yay! Here's Miss Cosy Con's Cosplay Dos & Don'ts for your Dante's Fire Con journey! Pay attention, cuties!

SLIDE #2: KA-BOOM! Keep those projectile weapons and laser-aiming devices or air cannons in check!

SLIDE #3: OUCHIE! NO swords, knives of any style, axes, hatchets, tomahawks, scythes, kunai, etc., including shuriken (throwing stars and darts!) unless properly padded!

SLIDE #4: OH LA LA! NO offering services in exchange for goods or fun favors! Tee hee!

SLIDE #5: CHOKING BAD! You may NOT lead another person around with leashes, handcuffs, chains, or ropes!

SLIDE #6: NAUGHTY BITS MUST BE COVERED! Costumes must be 'street-legal!' Bikini area must be covered on both men and women. No storming the beaches topless here, cuties!

SLIDE #7: NO bare feet! ... Don't be stupid.

SLIDE #8: WATCH YOUR WINGS! Costumes must be kept to a manageable size, 'o my darlings! This applies to wings and tails! Duh!

SLIDE #9: HOW MANY FINGERS AM I HOLDING UP? You must have a clear line of sight through those cosplay costume peepholes! Or a fellow cosplayer MUST act as a handler at all times. Yay friends!

SLIDE #10: DANTE'S FIRE CON *HEARTS* THE FOLLOWING! Replica weapons of wood, foam, plastic, resin, fiberglass, and non-metal training weapons!

SLIDE #11: HAPPY HUNTING! Bows and crossbows are awesome but must be kept in a quiver! Arrow tips! Bows should be loosely strung with a weak material like yarn. Yay, yarn!

SLIDE #12: Have a good Con and remember to always play safe, o' my darlings!

ACT ONE

Scene 1: Dante Never Gives Up

(Video projection #1: Anime music blares. A montage: Quick snippets of videos spliced together flash by. In the snippets that appear we see three teenage girls: **DANYA**, **HONEY**, *and* **ELLEN**. *They are dressed up as their favorite characters and cosplaying (acting out scenes) from their favorite anime/manga comic,* Dante's Fire. *The short video ends with* **ELLEN** *looking at the camera – at us. Video off. Lights out.)*

(Title projection up: GEEK!)

(Harsh lights snap up. **DANYA** *and* **HONEY** *shivering in the freezing cold. Their jackets and sweatshirts cover their cosplaying outfits, but hints of their costumes peek out.* **HONEY** *carries a large duffel bag.* **DANYA** *has a small bag slung across her shoulder. They are outside the convention center entrance; the door is open – casting a warm glow of light on them. But they anxiously face the burly thirty-something* **SECURITY GUARDS** *who are in their way, reviewing lists attached to their clipboards. These* **GUARDS** *do nothing for good or evil, just their job.)*

GUARD #1. You're not on the list.

DANYA. The hell we're not.

HONEY. Danya. Chill, okay. *(to* **GUARDS***)* Please, just look again, okay?

GUARD #2. We did.

DANYA. Well, look again. Maybe this time you'll remember how to read. We're there. Danya Spenser and –

HONEY. Roberta Taylor. I might be under Honey. It's a nickname that stuck.

GUARD #1. Sweet. But uh, yeah, you're not listed.

DANYA. We drove from Cleveland. Like five freaking hours!

GUARD #1. And that's how long you're gonna drive back.

HONEY. Please, we're here to see Joto Samagashi.

GUARD #2. And so is everyone at Dante Fire Con, whoever the heck he is.

DANYA. SHE created *Dante's Fire!* SHE'S the greatest manga and anime creator, like ever.

HONEY. *(to DANYA)* Uh, Tezuka – ? Astroboy.

DANYA. *(to HONEY)* Correction: greatest living manga creator ever.

GUARD #1. You. Are. Not. On. The. List. If we're wrong, show us your tickets.

DANYA. We paid months ago. There should be three tickets. Danya Spenser. Honey and –

HONEY. Ellen Taylor.

GUARD #2. Well we have an Ellen Taylor.

DANYA. That's us, jerk off!

GUARD #1. When she appears and shows her magical ID, I can use my magical powers of security guard-dom to let you in.

HONEY. She couldn't make it.

GUARD #2. Well then – you're going to have to go back around to the front of this glorious palace of a convention center and pay for this freak fest like every other weirdo.

DANYA. How much is it?

GUARD #2. 60 bucks a ticket.

HONEY. How much do we have Danya?

DANYA. After that lame rest stop where you ate like five whoppers –

HONEY. Like three! And one of them was a junior!

DANYA. We're wasting time! Please! There's only an hour and fifteen minutes left!

GUARD #2. How's that our fault? Who comes to one of these things on the last possible day!

HONEY. We had complications, okay?

DANYA. And we have to see Samagashi. It's important!

GUARD #1. Look, I get obsessions. I love to snuggle up with a good bottle of gin and The Wrath of Khan.

GUARD #2. *(correcting him – a heated subject)* Empire. Strikes. Back.

GUARD #1. Your mistake, my friend!

GUARD #2. No, the mistake is that you and I agreed to work an event populated by kids, lining up at 6 a.m., looking like Back to the Future slipped Mad Max a roofie and popped out some Stripe-Gremlins-Chud-Rosemary's Baby!

DANYA. What's Gremlins?

GUARD #1. This conversation is over.

HONEY. Wait! Please can't you do something to help – a fellow geek?

GUARD #1. Oh, a fellow geek, well. Jerry…

GUARD #2. What Tom?

GUARD #1. Should we give them a chance to prove they're worthy before crossing the Bridge of Death?

DANYA. Oh, c'mon.

(They eye each other. Standoff.)

GUARD #1. Where does Princess Leia tell Grand Moff Tarkin the rebel base is located?

*(**DANYA** and **HONEY** look at each other blankly at this old school geek lore.)*

GUARD #2. Dantoine!

*(**GUARDS** high five. **GUARD #2** takes role of "Quiz Host.")*

Yeah! Who appears in all five Trek shows?

GUARD #1. Majel Roddenberry! Gene's widow. The voice of the Trek computer! Hah!

(The GUARDS high five.)

GUARD #2. Feel the sting of our awesome!

GUARD #1. *(making bee stinging noise)* Zzzzzz! You lose Pikachus!

HONEY. Here! *(HONEY offers manga to GUARDS.)* This is one of *Dante's Fire's* best issues in the whole wide freakin' world! It's yours if you let us in.

(GUARD #1 takes the comic.)

GUARD #1. WOW! Now, I see. You're just in time! I need another good "Jokes for the John".

(GUARDS snicker. Why are they so mean?!)

HONEY. Hey!

GUARD #2. *(waving magazine)* Speaking of – nature calls!

GUARD #1. Goodbye girls!

DANYA. But Samagashi never shows up anywhere – this is our only chance!

HONEY. You don't understand – you don't –

(The GUARDS exit. The back door slams shut and the glowing light blinks out.)

DANYA. What the hell! Open this door! Freaking, lame-shit-ass jerk faces!

HONEY. Could you try being a little less angry?

DANYA. Well, anger is kinda my thing.

HONEY. Well, it's getting kinda old.

DANYA. What does that mean?

HONEY. What do you think it means? We're just sitting there, everyone in the living room, and you pull me aside out of nowhere – right there while my whole family is just … And then you're all, *(imitating DANYA)*

"I'm going. I need to get the convention. I need to take your parents' car!"

DANYA. It's not my fault my dad has a piece of crap Honda!

HONEY. Whatever happened to "we?" The whole ride over with your hood up (**HONEY** *pulls up her sweatshirt hood and imitates* **DANYA** *driving angry behind the wheel.*) saying nothing about her – like all you're doing is trying not to talk about it.

DANYA. You said you wanted to come with me.

HONEY. What am I supposed to say?

DANYA. That you know this is right! Everyone was just sitting around – No offense to you or your family, but Ellen would have hated everything about this weekend okay. And she wouldn't care, if I didn't want to talk about it.

HONEY. Actually, she would have... If you want to remember something that really happened instead of idealizing every single thing my sister did before she –

DANYA. You want to be here for the same reason I do.

(**DANYA** *holds up her bag – what's inside must be very important to them!*)

We do this Honey and then everything will be –

HONEY. Better? Okay? Is that really what you think?

DANYA. I think Dante never gives up.

(**DANYA** *takes out her iPhone. She presses play.* Dante's Fire *theme song triumphantly blares.*)

HONEY. Don't. Don't even –

(**DANYA** *dances around* **HONEY** *as the music gets louder.* **HONEY** *can't help but let out a laugh. Smiles.* **HONEY** *unzips her hoodie revealing her* **VIRGIE** *character outfit underneath. She plops on her pink, short hair wig or flicks her already short highlighted hair.* **VIRGIE**, *the character* **HONEY** *is cosplaying, is a spunky, go-to gal, full of gadgets, fun, and perhaps aviation goggles! After all she's a sassy pilot.* **DANYA** *grins throwing off* *her jacket revealing the Dante outfit she wears.* **DANTE** *is a character who fights first and talks later, but has unexpected humility at times, a bad ass ready for anything and his outfit reflects it. Though* **DANYA** *is playing a male character – she's also selected items that still show her femininity. She puts her hair in a pony tail.* **DANYA** *and* **HONEY** *grow more and more excited – diving into the large duffel bag they've brought, taking out items to complete their costumes.* **HONEY** *bows to* **DANYA**, *giving her a blue, plastic sword.* **DANYA** *smiles and bows back, takes it from her as if it were real. My goodness! Look!* **DANYA** *and* **HONEY** *have transformed before us into* **DANTE** *and* **VIRGIE**. *They're having so much fun they don't notice* **MARCY** *and* **MOLLY**, *dressed in black with huge devil wings and boots, sneaking up on them.* **DANYA** *and* **HONEY** *realize they're being watched. The music comes to a halt as they turn to face…)*

DANYA & HONEY. *Dante's Fire* Devil Angels!

MARCY. YAY! I told you it is them! The girls who acted out all the videos!

HONEY. You saw them?

MOLLY. We love them! *(Waving "hello." Introducing herself)* Molly!

MARCY. Marcy! We heard what the guards said to you. So mean!

MOLLY. Awful, stinky bad guards! Not like pretty Dante's Angels Super Sister Guardians of the Hell Universe. Do you think we're pretty?

*(**MOLLY** and **MARCY** pose.)*

HONEY. Sure!

MOLLY & MARCY. YAY!

*(**MOLLY** and **MARCY** run to **HONEY** and **DANYA**. They hug them tightly.)*

DANYA. That was fast.

MOLLY. Well everything happens faster these days with technology! We live in an accelerated culture you know. Every moment here is a life changing moment. *(pause)* Oh that was good!

MARCY. *(pulls out her phone and types)* Tweeted it!

DANYA. Look we don't have a lot of time. The convention's gonna close. Can you get us in?

MARCY. It's a insane cosplaying world in there! You can barely tell what's real and what's not.

MOLLY. *(handing* **HONEY** *a game cartridge)* It changes the way you see things.

DANYA. We're not scared of anything.

MARCY. No one ever is, baby. Until it gets shitballs crazy! Follow us!

(She puts out her hand and they all pile their hands on.)

ALL. GIRL POWER!!!

(They throw their hands up in the air as they jump up. **MOLLY** *and* **MARCY** *motion for* **DANYA** *and* **HONEY** *to follow them through a secret entrance into the con.)*

(Video projection #2: Intense rock music blares. A filmed advertisement of the convention plays! Images of a convention in progress – tons of people – toys – booths – flash by as **ANNOUNCER** *talks. NOTE: If video is limited, it is possible to stage this projection.)*

ANNOUNCER. WELCOME COLUMBUS, OHIO TO DANTE'S FIRE CON! FEATURING DANTE ANIME! DANTE MOVIES! DANTE COMICS! DANTE'S FIRE CON! THE ULTIMATE COSPLAYING CONVENTION THAT HAS IT ALL! ALL THE AWESOME COSPLAY YOU WANT, ALL THE TIME! NOW. NOW! NOW! From the best anime series of all time, created by the one and only, JOTO SAMAGASHI! This weekend only. Dante's Fire Con is created to replicate Dante's journey across the universe! Cosplay as your favorite characters in all nine *Dante's Fire* dimensions! This is where you'll catch 'em all!

(Images of the characters scroll by.)

ANNOUNCER. *(cont.)* Our hero Dante! Navigator Virgie! The evil Cleo! The slick Ulee-o! Cute Squeaker. And all the rest!

*(Image changes to a **FATHER** and his **KID**.)*

CLUELESS FATHER. Cosplaying? What's that?

GEEK KID. Cosplayers in Japan, called *reiya* or *kosupure*, are teens who dress up as characters they admire and gather together with other like-minded friends to engage in cosplay. The whole point is to become someone else in order to find yourself! The power of transformation is a huge thing in Japanese culture –

ANNOUNCER. But all YOU need to know is it's FREAKING awesome! All thanks to JOTO SAMAGASHI!

(Images of celebrities scroll and are voiced over.)

SAMUEL L. JACKSON. God Bless Joto Samagashi! Her animated TV shows – and *Dante's Fire* Energy Cereal Crunch! – are what gets me up in the morning and keeps me going!

GEORGE LUCAS. Every time I make another blue ray Wampa on Hoth I silently pray: Bless you. Joto Samagashi.

ANNOUNCER. And holy heck! She's here! Right inside Dante's Fire Con! Signing whatever your geek-filled heart desires!!!

(An image of Joto Samagashi in a baseball cap, her face obscured, trying not to be seen holding up her hand, is shown.)

The ever reclusive and exclusive Joto Samagashi the most influential manga creators of all time is our guest artist! DO YOU HEAR WHAT I'M FREAKING SAYING? SIGN UP NOW TO SEE HER! WHAT ARE YOU WAITING FOR? DON'T MESS THIS UP!! THIS IS THE LAST DAY! THE LAST HOUR! SUNDAY! SUNDAY! SUNDAY! FOR SAMAGASHI!

(an image of **COSPLAYERS** *gathered together happily shouting)*

COSPLAYERS. Abandon all hope! All ye who enter here!

(Film ends. Light up on **HONEY** *and* **DANYA** *who stand in the middle of the ever-busy-big-bad-wild-world of Dante's Fire Con.* **DANYA** *clutches her bag tightly. Everywhere they look there are cosplayers rolling dice, dancing and singing on stage, merchandise is being sold! Everyone is dressed up and going crazy.)*

HONEY. Oh, man.

DANYA. This place is more packed than Minotaur's Mega Metropolis.

HONEY. It is! But how are we gonna –

DANYA. Honey. We'll be the best Dante and Virgie, ever. And what does Virgie do?

HONEY. Right!

*(***HONEY*** holds up the USB device/cartridge* **MOLLY** *gave her. She takes out her own handheld DS game player and puts the device in. Suddenly* **MISS COSY,** *an animated projection of a cute girl cosplayer, designed to be an interactive guide to the con, appears projected on the wall behind them. NOTE:* **MISS COSY** *can also be a puppet, or appear live.)*

MISS COSY. Tee. Hee. Please INSERT NAMES.

HONEY. *(typing their names into her game player)* Oh!

MISS COSY. Hello! Pleased to meet you DANY-YA and HONE-Y! Welcome to all nine dimensions of Dante's quest!

*(***MISS COSY*** gestures to a map, which appears on the screen. It is horribly and wonderfully complicated and crazy.)*

See?! Pretty! Ms. Samagashi signs on the 9th level! But OMG, it's 5:45 and we close at 7 P.M. sharp!

HONEY. *(signing up)* Samagashi! C'mon we just want to sign up to see –

MISS COSY. Got it! Your number is: 465,783,231009,800, 6999 –

DANYA & HONEY. HOLY CRAP BALLS!

HONEY. Danya! How are we gonna get up there now?

(an elevator dings)

DANYA. The elevator!

(**DANYA** *and* **HONEY** *run to the elevator, which is offstage. However, teenagers, dressed like a Steampunk Army, spill out of the doors and onto the stage, stopping them.*)

STEAMPUNK LEUT #1. YO YO YO YO, these here elevators only run for Sir Major Ulee-o of the Steampunk Army of Hell!

STEAMPUNK LEUT #2. Yo.

DANYA. Well, we don't care "yo," we have to –

HONEY. Oh, my god, really? What? Ulee-o's my favorite character.

DANYA. I thought I was your favorite character.

HONEY. Next to you, of course. *(gesturing to others)* And you. And you. *(beat)* Yo.

STEAMPUNK LEUT #2. He's almost here. Yo! Clear the way! Clear the way for Major Ulee-o! Attention! Yo!

DANYA. Ah! I don't care if some geek dresses up like the hottest guy in the show just let us –

(The **LEUTS** *silence* **DANYA.** *They whip out a small boom box and play Ulee-o's theme song.)*

STEAMPUNK LEUTS.

HIS ARMOR SHINES LIKE THE SUN!
FREAKIN' AWESOME SINCE THE WORLDS BEGUN
HIS ROAD IS THE ROAD TO EVERYONE
ASHORE FROM THE DANGEROUS SEA-YO
IS FREAKIN' AWESOME, SIR MAJOR ULEE-O

(As they rap, **TOBY** *another teenager dressed as* **ULEE-O,** *enters with his back to the audience.)*

He is just!

(**TOBY** *turns around dramatically. Oh he is cute!*)

TOBY. He just is!

STEAMPUNK LEUTS #1 & #2.

HE MOVES THE HEAVENS!
HE IS A FREAKIN' WIZ!

STEAMPUNK LEUTS #1 & #2.

SO, FREAKIN' WISE!
THE CUTEST EYES!
MAKES LOVE PRIMAL!

TOBY. If you know what I mean.

STEAMPUNK LEUTS #1 & #2.

IF YOU DON'T LOVE HIM, YOU'RE JUST PLAIN CRAZY, GIRL!
DON'T BE STUPID! HE'S HERE! YO.
HE'S FREAKIN' AWESOME SIR MAJOR ULEE-OOO!

TOBY. Yo, my lady.

DANYA. "Yo, my lady" this Sir-Doche-A-Lot.

(**DANYA** *flips him the bird.*)

TOBY. Danya? Honey?

HONEY. Whoa! You do have mind powers.

TOBY. It's me. Toby from Brooklyn?

(*Breaking the suave act,* **TOBY** *jumps up and down happy to see them.*)

We played online! DF chat room.

(*aside to* **DANYA**) Ullee-o-251? C'mon. You sent me those fan videos you guys were making.

DANYA. And apparently you formed some kind of cult.

TOBY. We are the army Ulee-o himself once formed to govern the Universe!

DANYA. Look Toby –

TOBY. Danya. I… I've been trying to get in touch with you.

DANYA. We haven't been on line in a few days.

TOBY. About Ellen is it really true she –

DANYA. How do you – ?

TOBY. It's posted all over. I didn't even think you'd be here.

HONEY. Well, we are here ok!

TOBY. But –

DANYA. Look, we don't have time to banter with your double-dealingness, okay? Just let us use the elevators.

(She clutches her bag swung across her shoulder, reminding her of its importance.)

We have to see Samagashi!

TOBY. *(dramatically as* **ULEE-O***)* Only those ready for the truth can see Samagashi.

DANYA. We're not ready to see Samagashi and those geeks are?

TOBY. I'm saying I don't care about them.

(Beat. **TOBY** *smiles. He's so cute!* **DANYA** *resists!)*

DANYA. Just playing Ulee-o, huh. You never know if he's good or bad. So, why should I trust you?

TOBY. Everyone trusts me. I'm loveable.

*(***HONEY** *sighs.* **DANYA** *shoots her a look.)*

HONEY. It's true!

TOBY. Just know Samagashi will make time for you, if you make the time.

(The lighting suddenly becomes heightened-fantasy lighting, mimicking how our cosplayers "imagine" this moment. The **LEUTS** *dramatically make a magical noise as* **TOBY** *takes off a golden watch from around his neck and throws it to* **DANYA***. She catches it in awe. Harsh reality lights pop back on.* **DANYA** *stares at what he's given her.)*

'Til next time, o' my darling.

*(***TOBY** *dramatically exits.)*

STEAMPUNK LEUT #1. He's gone.

*(***STEAMPUNK LEUTS #1** *and* **#2** *exit.* **HONEY** *looks back to "timepiece.")*

HONEY. Cool! Dante's timepiece for magically jumping from porthole to porthole to descend to each ring!

DANYA. And how is a baby stroller wheel painted gold with an alarm clock glued onto it going to help us?

HONEY. Only the timekeeper knows how to work it anyway.

(*BRIAN, a creepy hooded kid dressed like the* **TIMEKEEPER** *enters.*)

BRIAN. Hello, I am here.

HONEY & DANYA. Timekeeper!

BRIAN. Steampunk Ulee-o is right you know. There is, uh, another way. To find –

DANYA. Samagashi?

BRIAN. Uh-huh. How good are your moves?

(*They do some moves.*)

Very good! "I choose you!"

HONEY. To do what?

(*We hear bloodthirsty cheers: "Fight! Fight! Fight!"*)

BRIAN. It's a secret.

(*BRIAN acting as Timekeeper touches the wall as if to open a magical, hidden door but in reality he is just opening a door leading to…*)

DANYA & HONEY. Ah! Emergency stairwell!

DANYA. For Samagashi.

HONEY. For Ellen.

(*They exit.*)

Scene 2: To the Victor Go the Spoils, Duh!

(In darkness we hear **MISS COSY**'s *voice reminding us...)*

MISS COSY. Tee hee! Just a reminder Con-sters! Here at Dante's Fire Con there is ABSOLUTELY NO MOCK FIGHTING! Weapons or props may NOT be wielded or brandished in a reckless manner. To do so is illegal and Miss Cosy will find you! Oh, yes, she will. Tee hee!

(Sound of cheering from a bloodthirsty crowd of geeks! Lights bump up on **DANYA** *and* **HONEY** *who are standing in some kind of ring!* **BRIAN** *and a crowd of cosplayers are heard or seen cheering around the ring.* **DANYA**'s *bag is still slung across her shoulder.)*

DANYA & HONEY. Battledome!

*(***BRIAN**, *still acting like the* **TIMEKEEPER**, *throws padded "American Gladiator"-like-huge-jousting-foam-sticks at* **DANYA** *and* **HONEY**, *which they catch.)*

DANYA. Whoa!

HONEY. Danya – listen! I have a feeling–

DANYA. That we can totally do this, right?!

HONEY. *(to* **TIMEKEEPER***)* Is that true? If we win, we'll meet Samagashi?

BRIAN. Dudes! I'm the Timekeeper. I make magical stuff happen all the time. Yes, totally. You win, you get an express trip to hell – and Samagashi.

CROWD. Samagashi! Samagashi!

BRIAN. Timekeeper says: It's TIME!!! First fight! Three jabs wins!

DANYA. Just follow me, ok?

HONEY. I can take care of myself, you know!

(The ground rumbles! Someone or something is coming...)

Uh – Danya – ?!

BRIAN. First out of the air duct grate gate!

(BRIAN gestures to a little gate that leads to an air duct [or gestures to the wings].)

Minotaur!!!

(Fantasy lighting. Footsteps grow louder! The ground shakes! DANYA and HONEY prepare to fight. Lighting returns to normal when MINNIE, dressed like a MINOTAUR, an overzealous geek, jumps out with a jousting stick.)

MINNIE. Every geek for themselves! It's the only way. The best geek wins the best geek – gets led straight down to see Samagashi before this place closes for all TIME, right Brian?!

BRIAN. I told you – I'm Timekeeper! We're not at Masque and Mime Drama Camp right now, Minnie!

HONEY. Wait. What grade are you in?

BRIAN. Fifth.

DANYA. How does a fifth grader end up running an illegal cosplay fight club?

BRIAN. Who are you to question me? Are you smarter than a fifth grader?

DANYA. Yes! *(to HONEY)* All we have to do is win. Easy, right?

MINNIE. Wrong! I'll crush you! I know all of minotaur's moves. I've been working on 'em. I love the ladies. I love the cheeseburgers. I love my *Dante's Fire* glow in the dark underroos – you know, the one with Ulee-o and Dante flying through the stars and Cleo following them with her red ax of fire. I'm ready to go in! To win! To go straight down. To see Samagashi! I'm ready!

HONEY. Wow, you really love Samagashi, too.

MINNIE. YES! Took the bus. The bus broke down. Found a car. Smashed through. Don't know how to drive. Got out of the car. Ran. Little old lady found me – thought I looked cute and petted me and called me Maxie poo and I let her. I let her. Door opened. Ran out. Guards. So mean. Wanted money. So much money. Ran to

ATM. Ate my card. Kicked it. Screamed. Calmed.
Thought: What would Samagashi do? Sold my entire
Dante's Fire first series right there in front of those Geek
Gestapo. Said they needed exact change. Ran to deli.
Got banana. Potassium! Ran back. Threw the money.
Ran. And now victory! I'm ready to win now, Brian!

BRIAN. Timekeeper!

MINNIE. For Samagashi!!!

*(Fantasy lighting. **DANYA** and **MINNIE** fight in slow
motion. **DANYA** easily wins. Lights snap back to reality.
MINNIE is crushed.)*

Bus fare?

*(**DANYA** and **HONEY** shake their heads "no." **MINNIE**
exits, defeated, back into the grate.)*

DANYA. We won! Take us to Samagashi.

BRIAN. You won. *(about **HONEY**)* This one didn't fight.

HONEY. That's not fair!

BRIAN. Don't worry you'll get your chance. With your arch
rival – reigning champion CLEO!

*(**GWEN** bounces out of the grate. She is dressed like
CLEO, the villain from the series. She waves her huge,
jousting-padded ax, and does some super sassy cheer-
leader-like moves.)*

GWEN. Go. Fight. Win! YEAH!

DANYA. What the hell kind of moves are that?

GWEN. Super sexy death battle awesome time moves Danya-
Dorcus!

(She attacks them as they battle/chat.)

DANYA. Gwen Sweetiny!

HONEY. You know her?

DANYA. Before I transferred.

GWEN. Are you going to even try to fight Danya-Dorcus?

DANYA. We're not on the playground – I'm not twelve –
you have no right to call me that here!

GWEN. Oh, come on, Karate Kid, I was never that bad. Ever since I met Toby playing online, I realized I can save my aggression for this!

(GWEN *does a big attack with her ax joust.*)

DANYA. *(defending against* GWEN*)* Toby?

GWEN. *(circling around* DANYA, *twirling her ax)* Toby's my boyfriend so – We share. He loves my videos. My dad. He helped me with the green screen – played Squeaker in the live action movie –

HONEY. I LOVE SQUEAKER! Your dad really plays him?

GWEN. Yeah – we have his whole orange furry outfit on the tenth floor.

HONEY. Wow, you live in a mansion?!

DANYA. HONEY! If you're too scared to fight then please shut up!

HONEY. I'm not scared!

GWEN. You should be – of the government! Universal health care right?! That's what my dad says.

DANYA. If your dad is so awesome Gwen-dorkus then why the hell are you here – why doesn't he just get you in to see Samagashi?

GWEN. Industry people are busy – that's what makes them better than us. And he has to work the Squeaker booth – I mean – it's not his weekend to see me anyway. And who cares?! Then I get to spend more time with Toby. We texted all last summer – sometimes texting all night long!

DANYA. You are a pale imitation to Ellen's Cleo. You don't deserve to see Samagashi. *(to* HONEY*)* C'mon Honey – we'll find another way.

(DANYA *turns to go.*)

GWEN. Oh yeah?! HAH!

(GWEN *pushes the backside of her axe into* DANYA's *back, shoving her to the ground.*)

DANYA. Ah!

HONEY. Hey! Leave her alone.

*(**HONEY** swats **GWEN** with her jousting stick.)*

YES! Virgie's going to kick your butt!

*(**GWEN** stands, angry. She raises her axe.)*

DANYA. *(struggling to get up)* Honey –

HONEY. *(jumping in front of **DANYA**)* I got this!

*(**GWEN** attacks **HONEY** who defends, fights back. **GWEN** isn't all talk – she's good. **HONEY** holds her own, but suddenly gets hurt! **DANYA** jumps back into the fight. She knocks **GWEN** to the ground. **GWEN** panics and changes up the game.)*

GWEN. Tag team!

*(**BRIAN**, as Timekeeper, blows a whistle. A kid with headgear dressed in a weird, metallic, robotic outfit enters.)*

HONEY, DANYA, & GWEN. Fifth Dimension Fire Bot-Boy!

BOT-BOY. Uh-huh. I was taught to respect all life forms. You girls are pretty.

(Girls go "Awww.")

And I'm so sorry I have to hurt you. But you flesh-babes gotta be taught some responsibility.

*(Big Robot fight – they are almost crushed. In the fight **BOT-BOY** gets **DANYA**'s bag.)*

HONEY. No!

BOT-BOY. Bot Boy senses something special inside.

GWEN. Bring it to me. To the Victor go the spoils, duh Danya Dorkus! Hah!

*(He hands **GWEN** the bag, and she waves it around, taunting.)*

Who's winning now?! Who always wins?

DANYA. Give it back or … *(tossing aside cosplay joust sticks)* or I'm going to kick your ass for real.

GWEN. Wow. Dark. Maybe it is true what Ellen said –

DANYA. What do you mean?

GWEN. You have gone off the deep end.

DANYA. Ellen talked to you?

GWEN. Everyone in the chatroom was talking about what happened after we found out what Ellen did. She was saying for weeks how she didn't even want to be friends with you anymore. Ellen said all you wanted to do was cosplay this all the time, and you didn't care what happened to her after you posted those videos. There were all those comments. God. Still, you go out and act like – well, you were just asking for a long deserved beating.

DANYA. Leave me alone.

GWEN. Why do you think she killed herself?

DANYA. Shut up!

GWEN. She didn't want to play anymore and you couldn't handle it.

DANYA. I said SHUT THE HELL UP!!!

(**DANYA** *hits* **GWEN***! It's violent and intense – surprising all of them! The bag falls to the floor.*)

HONEY. Oh, my god.

(*Clearly shaken,* **DANYA** *grabs back her bag.*)

GWEN. You hurt my nose you freak!

DANYA. I didn't mean to –

(**HONEY** *grabs* **BRIAN**.)

HONEY. Look we won your dumb game – take us to Samagashi!

BRIAN. I can't. I was just making this up!

HONEY. You mean we did this for nothing?

BRIAN. You think I don't want to meet Samagashi?! We all do. At least I gave us hope.

DANYA. There is never hope in lying.

(**BRIAN** *runs off crying.*)

HONEY. Danya! You're bleeding!

(Flashlights! The **GUARDS** *rush in.)*

GUARD TWO. What kind of Death Star hellhole insanity is going on in here?!

*(***GWEN*** points at them.)*

GWEN. It's their fault. Those crazy freaks started it all!

*(***HONEY*** grabs **DANYA**. *Everyone is after them.)*

DANYA. The air duct!

HONEY. Danya!

*(***HONEY*** grabs **DANYA**. *They flee through the air duct, closing the gate behind them. Blackout.)*

Scene 3: Another Way In

(Video projection #3: One of the videos the girls have made is projected. While home-made and put together by filming each other in their backyard, using home-made props of course, the videos are impressive and inventive. The videos consist of jump cuts between different scenes. Here **DANYA** *cosplays* **DANTE** *and* **ELLEN** *cosplays* **CLEO***. At the start* **ELLEN** *is playing* **CLEO** *before she turns evil.)*

DANYA. Are you sure I am the one to hold the sword of fire?

(Cut to: **DANYA** *walking alongside* **ELLEN** *as their characters.)*

Cleo. I have to go with Ulee-o and his army – he's the only one who can lead me to the center of the universe. The tower.

ELLEN. You choose him over me?

DANYA. I have to go! You have to stay here and make sure our village is safe.

(Cut to: close up of **ELLEN** *playing* **CLEO** *and* **DANYA** *playing* **DANTE** *shouting in each other's face. This shot captures that "split- screen-anime-yelling face feeling.")*

ELLEN. You'd abandon your best friend?! Who has fought beside you?

DANYA. You can't come.

ELLEN. Why?

DANYA. Because friends get in the way and I don't want you to get in my way, okay?!

ELLEN. I hate you!

DANYA. I don't hate you, but you have to seriously chill! I'll be back for you I promise.

(Cut to: **ELLEN** *as* **CLEO** *picks up a homemade prop that represents a huge powerful crystal (something like a box lined with tin foil with a light inside so it glows as she peers in).)*

ELLEN. Yes. Ah! Oh, no, what's – THE POWER!!!

(ELLEN acts like CLEO turning evil! Directly at camera.)

I feel different. ALIVE! DANTE I'M COMING FOR YOU.

(Video out. Tick. Tick. Tick. Time is running out! Lights up on harsh reality. HONEY and DANYA crawl out of the grate into a bathroom. Stalls. Sounds of dripping. The bathroom is gloomy and they both are affected by the task they've come here to do and the violence that has just passed.)

HONEY. Oh, god – where are we?

DANYA. Miss Cosy.

HONEY. Right! Miss Cosy!

(HONEY takes out her game system and turns on MISS COSY, who is projected behind them. During this, DANYA stands, getting herself together, swinging her bag across her shoulder again.)

MISS COSY. Oh, I got so sleepy you weren't using me, you silly girls! Danya. Honey. What are you doing in the third floor bathroom? Why aren't you out having fun?

DANYA. Because I'm bleeding, Miss Cosy!

MISS COSY. How can you be glum when there's Cotton Candy Land on this floor at Squeaker's Candy Corner!

HONEY. Squeaker!

DANYA. Honey! We don't care about that right now – we need to find a way out of here!

HONEY. There isn't a way out, Danya.

(HONEY grabs DANYA's hand, trying to clean up her cut and bandage it.)

You can only get out using the main floors. We go out there and they'll catch us for sure. Look at you. Don't you ever just think –

DANYA. People get mad, Honey. People screw up. People do horrible things. You start thinking – life gets complicated. Okay? Time runs out. Time is running out. C'mon. We have to go.

HONEY. You're not going anywhere until –

(**HONEY** *stops her, taking* **DANYA***'s arm which is bleeding.* **HONEY** *takes care of* **DANYA***'s wound while she talks.*)

– hold still! You're always so impatient.

DANYA. Do I have a choice?

HONEY. We all have choices. This is crazy. God. Coming here like – it won't change anything.

DANYA. That's Honey talking.

HONEY. What if I don't want to play Virgie right now, okay?

DANYA. You don't have to do anything you don't want to do, Honey. The last thing I want is for you to feel...

HONEY. What that Gwen girl said, do you think –

DANYA. No. Ellen loved playing this more than anything.

HONEY. Where are you going?

DANYA. To see Samagashi. Are you coming?

HONEY. We can't just walk out there now! They're waiting for us!

DANYA. A hero doesn't think – a hero does! You can't be scared, Honey –

HONEY. What the hell? You, you're going to teach me now? When you can't even tell me why – ?

DANYA. No one can. It happened. *(hesitant to bring it up)* And I have one more year here and then I graduate and –

HONEY. You're saying this right now? Out of all the possible things –

(**HONEY** *goes into one of the stalls, closes the door.* **DANYA** *holds the bag in front of her, trying to find the right words. She softly speaks through the bathroom door to* **HONEY**.)

DANYA. Honey. Look. Ellen – she'd worry about you. Calling out sick just to avoid going to class? That's not you. You have to stand up for yourself.

HONEY. Don't tell me what my sister –

DANYA. She knew that you can't keep acting like a kid.

HONEY. And you can't keep acting like you don't care!

DANYA. Being here now is caring. Getting this to Samagashi is caring.

HONEY. For you. Not for her. That's the truth, isn't it? This is all about you!

DANYA. How can you say that? Seriously. Grow up, Honey.

HONEY. Me? Look at you!

(Sound of purring. **DANYA** *stops* **HONEY** *from talking.)*

DANYA. Uh, Honey – I don't think we're alone.

(Flush! Two sets of feet donning high heeled red boots appear under the stalls. And then cat tails.)

DANYA & HONEY. *Dante's Fire* Devil Cats!

(Door stalls slam open and the cat ladies enter, wearing furry tails and high heeled red boots rimmed with fur. They are dressed in red tights and wear long gloves with claw-like nails they click together.)

DEVIL CAT #1. TICK.

DEVIL CAT #2. TICK.

DEVIL CAT #1. TICK. Time is running out. Ohhh. Joto.

DEVIL CAT #2. Samagashi.

DEVIL CAT #1. Have you seen those escalators?

DEVIL CAT #2. Packed.

DEVIL CAT #1. Such a shame.

DEVIL CAT #2. And the elevators are Steampunk Army express only, if you haven't noticed.

DANYA. Already noted. Do you only state the obvious?

DEVIL CAT #1. Don't rush a Devil Cat.

HONEY. We're in the bathroom. You can drop the act.

DEVIL CAT #2. What act? This is really us.

DEVIL CAT #1. Our alter egos work in another world.

DEVIL CAT #2. Receptionist.

DEVIL CAT #1. Office Manager.

DEVIL CAT #2. Filing.

DEVIL CAT #1. Emails.

DEVIL CAT #2. Deadlines.

HONEY. Wait a minute. You think being you is, um, when you're not pretending?

DEVIL CAT #2. Have you ever twitched a furry tail between your legs and seen who you end up with at the end of the night of these dreadful affairs?

HONEY. Uh – I'm thirteen.

DEVIL CAT #1. Well, crash course! It's awesome.

HONEY. Danya – ?

DEVIL CAT #2. Not used to us are you?

DANYA. You're different that's for sure.

DEVIL CAT #1. You can say it.

DEVIL CAT #2. Older.

DEVIL CAT #1. Late thirties!

DEVIL CAT #2. Shhhh. Don't tell.

DEVIL CAT #1. We can drink –

DEVIL CAT #2. Legally!

DEVIL CAT #1. And do drugs!

DEVIL CAT #2. Illegally!

DEVIL CAT #1. And order lots and lots of killer boots from Zappos!

DEVIL CAT #2. That we decoupage with our own cat's fur. *(showing off her furry boots)* Meow!

DEVIL CAT #1. But happiness?

DANYA. Is dressing up.

DEVIL CAT #2. Purrrrr. I like you.

DANYA. I see.

DEVIL CAT #1. We have experienced – so many cons.

DEVIL CAT #2. Cosplay.

DEVIL CAT #1. Fur fan clubs.

DEVIL CAT #2. You –

DEVIL CAT #1. Remind us –

DEVIL CAT #2. Of us.

DEVIL CAT #1. We might help you.

DEVIL CAT #2. If you show us.

DEVIL CAT #1. Why you're here.

DEVIL CAT #2. What's in the bag, Dante?

(**DANYA** *clutches her bag.*)

DANYA. It's private.

DEVIL CAT #1. Special?

DEVIL CAT #2. Valuable! Do tell.

DANYA. Private. For us. Stay away.

DEVIL CAT #2. But it's worthless unless you see her, isn't that right?

DEVIL CAT #1. We could take you there.

HONEY. You know how to get to Samagashi?

DEVIL CAT #1. We know another way in.

(**DEVIL CATS** *open a door! Or a hatch in the floor. Or gesture off stage! Something impressive! The girls peer in.*)

Exhibit Room A.

DEVIL CAT #2. The museum.

DANYA. C'mon, Honey – let's go.

(**DANYA** *exits into the museum.* **HONEY** *follows but one of the* **DEVIL CATS** *grabs* **HONEY**'s *shoulder, pulls her back and purrs in her ear.*)

DEVIL CAT #2. She only thinks of herself.

DEVIL CAT #1. She doesn't appreciate you.

DEVIL CAT #2. She has no right to see Samagashi.

DEVIL CAT #1. But you do little one.

DEVIL CAT #2. Remember in *Dante's Fire* real friends share.

HONEY. You want to be friends?

(*They cackle.*)

DEVIL CAT #1. Sure. You get us that precious bag. And we'll take you to Samagashi.

HONEY. You will?

DEVIL CAT #1. We'll find you. Meow.

DEVIL CAT #2. Chow.

> *(The* **DEVIL CATS** *smile big freaky cat smiles.* **HONEY** *breaks away from them and exits through the special entrance. The* **DEVIL CATS** *exit on the opposite side, cackling. Lights down.)*

Scene 4: How Do You Know You're Winning?

(Lights up on **DANYA** *standing in the middle of the hall.* **HONEY** *runs after her friend, skidding to a stop to avoid crashing into her. A slower, more heartfelt version of the* Dante's Fire *theme music plays as* **DANYA** *and* **HONEY** *look out in amazement at this place.)*

DANYA. Wow.

HONEY. OMG. So much Samagashi stuff.

Bibs, puzzles, all the toys! Uh, a rocking chair? Oh! The Sword of Fire! Look!

*(***HONEY** *opens her game system.* **MISS COSY***'s voice is heard.)*

MISS COSY. Welcome to Exhibit Hall A, the Samagashi Museum. Enter the exhibit number to learn more about the amazing objects you see.

*(***HONEY** *types numbers into the device.)*

Selection 51. What you see before you is Samagashi's first printed manga, or graphic novel. *Dante's Fire* First Edition. Samagashi first drew Dante after reading The Inferno in school at the tender age of ten. In her own words:

(We hear Samagashi's voice speaking in Japanese, as **MISS COSY** *translates over her)*

"I closed this masterpiece and looked out the window. Outside I saw a bright red bird in a tree and I imagined! What if that was a boy trying to get free from everyone who didn't understand him, who didn't care, his parents who could never see Dante was the one to fight to bring all the stars together – the hope that was stolen. I saw how, with this story, I could find peace in the world – "

HONEY. – and all the answers of the universe.

DANYA. She had a vision. Knew what she wanted every step of the way. It's when things are unclear – when we don't know where to go – that's when we get lost and …

(HONEY points up at a picture of Samagashi.)

HONEY. She looks so young, not much older than us. Ellen loves this picture…loved, she loved this picture. We would always –

DANYA. Samagashi had nothing. She had to fight for everything she got at Tenuso Studio. Just to be heard! That line – if only I could write like that! That *Dante's Fire* catch phrase was real for her: "I will go to the depth of hell for you, o' my darling!" Every time I hear that! I know it's not just Dante fighting, but me! When I play Dante. Fighting forever…for who I care about – I'll win, even if it's just me, I'll win because I can – because I have to –

(HONEY notices DANYA has let the grip on her bag loosen.)

HONEY. You know what? You're right. People do horrible things. Hurt those they love. But maybe they're just – growing up.

DANYA. What do you…?

(GWEN followed by the GUARDS bursts onto the stage. HONEY snatches the bag from the DANYA. They split – DANYA on one side of the stage – HONEY on the other, facing the intruders who stand between them.)

GWEN. That's them! They're crazy – tried to really hurt me. Not to mention cut in line and traumatized for that kid playing battle-bot boy for life!

GUARD ONE. And snuck in! That's them all right!

GWEN. Just that Dante cosplayer – Danya Spensor – she's the ringleader.

DANYA. Honey! Help!

(They grab DANYA. HONEY stands there, gripping the bag. Lighting focuses on DANYA and HONEY.)

Honey what are you doing? Do something!

HONEY. I am doing something. You remember that episode where Virgie turned against Dante in the crystal rock pit?

DANYA. "Crossing the Line, Episode 57" – the beach towel of it is right over there –

HONEY. Virgie knows what she wants. Knows what's right. You don't deserve to see Samagashi.

(Lights snap back to normal. **HONEY** *runs off with the bag.)*

DANYA. Honey, please! Come back! God damn it!

GUARD ONE. Lord's name in vain. That's not nice.

DANYA. Then how's this YOU JESUS H. CHRIST EFFING FREAKING IDIOTS!

*(***DANYA*** *goes crazy rushing the* **GUARDS.** *Lights go fantasy red, pulsing! Angry music plays! In a sudden flash of white light,* **GUARD #1** *grabs* **DANYA** *using a Vulcan nerve pinch. She falls dramatically to the floor, fine but knocked out. Lights return to normal. In reality* **GUARD #1** *seems a little unnerved that his Star Trek geekery has had such an effect, and looks down at her thoughtfully. These kids really take this character stuff seriously!* **GUARD #2** *is much less philosophical, raising her arms in an immediate declaration of triumph.)*

GUARD TWO. Yeah! Good wins over Evil, again! Trek or Wars we can agree on that, right friend?

*(***GUARD #1*** *takes out the comic book* **HONEY** *gave him in the first scene. He's clearly been reading it! He carefully hands it to* **GUARD #2** *who looks at him puzzled.)*

GUARD #1. I wish I could, but these kids – these kids dress up to BLUR the distinctions between machine and person, between male and female, reality and fantasy, good and evil. *Dante's Fire* leaves its characters groping to find their moorings. *(gestures to the incapacitated* **DANYA** *lying on the floor)* Dante wants to be happy, but only he has the answer, if he ever realizes his or her real power. *(He gestures to* **GWEN** *who is texting.)* Cleo plays the Villain because she thinks Dante's betrayed her, but in reality, it's because she's frightened of who she wants to become. *(looking off to where* **HONEY** *ran off)*

And Virgie – she can lead anyone where they want to go, but doesn't know where to go herself.

GUARD #2. But Star Wars and Star Trek rule cuz you know who's good and bad!

GUARD #1. Ah, but Spock himself would ask – does *Dante's Fire* go deeper? Look at this girl. She'll do anything to see Samagashi. If she's the hero, that makes us –

GUARD #2. What are you saying? Are you saying we're evil? How can we be evil if we're winning?

GUARD #1. The point is – how do we know we're winning?

(Suddenly, the lights change to a near blackout with a greenish tinge.)

GUARD #2. *Hey!*

*(The **GUARDS** and **GWEN** reach out unable to see. **TOBY** enters with glasses that light up. He has a blow dart device with a little red laser pointer on it, showing us where he's aiming...)*

GUARD #1. *(whimpering)* Who turned out the lights? *(seeing a red laser pointer on him)* Oh!

*(**TOBY** blows his dart gun and takes care of **GUARD #1**! Then **GUARD #2**! He chuckles to himself, pleased.)*

TOBY. Ah-hah, yo!

GWEN. *(recognizing his voice in the dark)* Toby. We're like totally going out what are you doing?

TOBY. Gwen. Texting does not a going-steady courtship make!

*(He bonks her on the head. She lands in his arm. He gently lies her down, then turns to **DANYA**.)*

How's that for showing what I can do, my lady?

DANYA. Took you long enough. Now let's go-Go-GO!

(They run offstage together.)

End Act One

ACT TWO

Scene 1: Imagining Together

(Video projection #4: **DANYA** *cosplays* **DANTE** *and* **HONEY** *cosplays* **VIRGIE** *in the story of how their characters met. Filmed in* **HONEY**'s *backyard. In this scene in the video,* **DANYA** *as* **DANTE** *is entangled by vines that are "alive" trying to eat her [to portray this they do something fun like cover* **DANYA** *with vines from plants from* **HONEY**'s *family's garden – she struggles pretending they are alive].* **HONEY** *as* **VIRGIE** *comes across this while out walking eating an apple with something she pretends is a staff.)*

DANYA. I don't need help, okay.

HONEY. Hmmm. You sure look like you do, unless you want those poisonous vines to eat you.

DANYA. Stupid vines.

HONEY. Hey! That's what keeps my planet alive. Shush, little ones.

(She pulls a little flute out of her pocket and plays a song to sooth them. **DANYA** *as* **DANTE** *is impressed.)*

I'm Virgie. And this is my furgly! SQUEAKER!

(Cut to: A little orange stuffed furry animal that **HONEY** *makes jump and hiss at* **DANYA** *or a picture of* **SQUEAKER**'s *she's drawn that she holds out. Then cut back to:* **DANYA**'s *face.)*

DANYA. *(sarcastically)* Charming pet.

(Cut to: **HONEY** *trailing behind* **DANYA** *as she walks.)*

HONEY. And of course everyone knows Dante.

DANYA. And apparently no one knows how to reach the tower of hell fire.

HONEY. I might – know – if you let me come with you!!!

DANYA. FINE! But only if you ALWAYS DO WHAT I SAY?!

HONEY. Deal!

(Cut to: ELLEN cosplaying CLEO trying to turn VIRGIE evil! ELLEN holds out the "crystal" box from the previous video. DANYA cosplaying DANTE rushes in.)

DANYA. Virgie stop!

ELLEN. Do it. Take the crystal Virgie – Join me! – what has Dante ever given you? Thanks to him you're stuck in this hell pit. Doomed forever. And for what? To save mankind? The most base of all creatures.

(HONEY takes the crystal.)

DANYA. No you can't, Virgie!

HONEY. I don't care what it does to me.

(turning evil and turning on DANYA)

It's what it does to you!

DANYA. No. Virgie – it's the crystal – it's making you –

ELLEN. Look like you're… constipated. Seriously, what the hell kinda face is that?

(They all crack up.)

DANYA. C'mon get it together girls! The con's in just two weeks!

ALL. For Samagashi!

(Video out. Sound of the clock. Tick! Tick! Tick! Harsh reality lights snap up on DANYA and TOBY in the elevator. It's packed with costumed characters including a GIRL AND BOY GOTH dressed like Dante's Fire Princesses. Elevator music is abruptly interrupted as MISS COSY's comes on giving an important announcement.)

MISS COSY. Tee hee! It's me Miss Cosy. Just a half hour until closing cosplayers! Last chance for all your hopes and dreams, my darlings! Oh goodness! NOW!!! This just in! Be on the lookout for the naughty Danya Spensor and Honey Taylor giving Dante and Virgie a very bad name! Oh, naughty bad-lings will be brought to Justice! Never fear, we shall find you! Tee hee!

(Everyone in the elevator stares at **DANYA***.)*

GOTH BOY PRINCESS. O.M.G. Are you –

*(***DANYA*** winces! Did they recognize her? Are they going to turn her in? Goths turn to* **TOBY***.)*

– wearing pure Australian leather? Did you make that yourself? It's so hot!

TOBY. Of course.

GOTH BOY PRINCESS. And the boots.

TOBY. And the laces, too.

GOTH GIRL PRINCESS. Oh! They're amazing.
You're amazing. We've always wanted to ride with you.

(They are fanning themselves going crazy.)

DANYA. Oh, god.

TOBY. What?

DANYA. Just because wannabe Princesses Arca and Aba think you're hot stuff –

GOTH GIRL PRINCESS. You're one to talk! A girl Dante? Seriously? Only "crossplay" girl babies dressed by their single mommies look like you.

DANYA. I totally dress myself, and I'm more Dante than Dante. So, watch out jerk-offs!

GOTH BOY PRINCESS. You're the jerk-off!

DANYA. Hey!

TOBY. Well, I see you make friends wherever you go.

DANYA. Look thanks for helping out, but I don't need help. Or friends.

TOBY. Why?

DANYA. Because friends get in the way and I don't want you to get in my way, okay?!

GOTH BOY PRINCESS. I knew I recognized you!

DANYA. Wait! That "Wanted" thing is so not –

GOTH GIRL PRINCESS. You're one of the girls that acted out all the episodes! Danya! Honey! Elle –

DANYA. Yeah. Well you know sometimes friends get really close and make some stupid videos and it ruins their lives.

TOBY. You don't really feel that way.

DANYA. How do you know what I feel?

(The elevator stops suddenly.)

What the hell?

GOTH BOY PRINCESS. It's been getting stuck all freaking weekend!

GOTH GIRL PRINCESS. I'm starving.

GOTH BOY PRINCESS. You cannot eat, if you want to stay in that dress.

DANYA. *(so frustrated at the situation – an outburst)* Ahhh!

TOBY. Look, if you're so upset just tell me where you want to go.

DANYA. I don't know! I have to find Honey – she ran off – I don't even know where she is! I have to find her. She's just a kid.

TOBY. Why did she run off?

DANYA. How should I know?

TOBY. Maybe if you stopped being so angry you would.

DANYA. I don't have time NOT to be angry. You run these elevators, don't you?

TOBY. I can't predict when they're going to break down. Just take a second and breathe.

GOTH GIRL PRINCESS. Ohhh, damn girl you should just kiss him now!

(They make kissy noises.)

DANYA. *(outburst)* Ah!

TOBY. Do they disturb you that much? Hey. Look at me.

DANYA. Why?

TOBY. Just concentrate on me.

DANYA. You're creeping me out!

TOBY. So, there's nothing else. Let time stop. Focus on your favorite place to be.

DANYA. This isn't a game.

TOBY. That's the problem. It's only by letting your mind go a little, that you can go anywhere. Focus. Where do you really want to be – *(imitating* ULEE-O*)* right now.

*(*TOBY *makes a dramatic, magical motion to* DANYA*'s forehead [acting like* ULEE-O *in the TV show]. Fantasy lighting fills the stage. The other costumed teens turn perfectly still, then exit as if pulled from this universe.* TOBY *and* DANYA *are now in their own world, which has a magical, airy feel. Images of flowers and Japanese landscapes are projected onto the walls around them. Sounds of Japanese music.)*

DANYA. Wow. Cafes. Little shops –

TOBY. – cherry trees – nice! I've never been to Japan.

DANYA. It's just this little village where my mom grew up – like she'd ever talk about it. Wait! How are you –.? How are you doing that? How can you see what I'm seeing? Did you slip me some drugs or something?

TOBY. We're imagining together. We can go any place.

(He goes to make his dramatic motion again, but DANYA *smacks his hand aside at the last second.)*

DANYA. Oh, god, this is so stupid. Why am I even sharing this with you?

TOBY. Because for a second you didn't care what other people think.

DANYA. I never do!

TOBY. We all do.

*(*TOBY *"sweeps" the projected images setting aside. He makes a gesture ushering in a new projection:* TOBY*'s*

school. We hear the sounds of a crowd watching a football game.)

DANYA. This is the football field at your school? We're in what you're imagining!

TOBY. Because you walk across it at lunch – you hear the same things. The same words. I learned how to deal with it.

DANYA. What are you – ?

(Fight music up! **TOBY** *faces* **DANYA.** *A sword is held up for him to grab from the wings. He does. He gets into a fighting position.)*

No way. I'm not fighting you.

TOBY. You fight everyone. You had no problem taking on Gwen.

DANYA. You mean your girlfriend!

TOBY. Nice. Now, show me what you can do, Dante.

DANYA. I don't want to hurt you but –

*(***DANYA*** reaches into the wings and gets her sword!)*

Hah!

(They race towards each other hitting each other with the first move! As they fight, they flirt.)

TOBY. Smooth.

DANYA. It's nice to know you can put that pretty outfit to use.

TOBY. Clothes don't make the man.

DANYA. What about the boy?

TOBY. Boyfriend – ?

DANYA. I told you, I don't need friends. That includes stupid boy-friends. Besides no guy could ever keep up with me.

TOBY. How am I doing – ?

DANYA. I just need more time.

TOBY. What about now – ?

DANYA. Better. But you're still a disappointment.

TOBY. And that's how you see the world.

DANYA. Fighting against it got me where I am.

(**TOBY** *bests* **DANYA** *and she falls to the floor.*)

TOBY. And how's that working out? Friendless and alone? Is that really what you want?

DANYA. Like you know anything about me!

(She goes to leave. **TOBY** *changes the setting. A forest setting. Night. We hear little sounds of little monsters, played by puppets, all around them. They can bounce and fly around them. The forest glows with them.* **DANYA** *runs to the little creatures, stays.)*

The forest of Gurgies! I love these Tiny wise monsters! *(beat)* Samagahi. I've got to meet her.

TOBY. Why?

DANYA. You don't want to?

TOBY. I don't know. *(shrugs)*

DANYA. You're afraid.

TOBY. Ulee-o is never afraid.

DANYA. Everyone is. So frightened to get what they really want.

TOBY. And what do you want… Danya?

(beat)

DANYA. I love it here – this is the one place I love. Wish it was real. Don't you?

TOBY. For me, here, I'm more like Toby than when I'm trying to be –

DANYA. *(teasing)* Ulee-o!

TOBY. Yeah. It's fun, but – sometimes I just want to be – Toby – you know? Danya?

DANYA. I'd rather be Dante than Danya any day. Every day. He won't ever stop. He keeps going until he makes things right. Makes mistakes, but he always tries for his friends. Trying to be this. It's the only way I know how to –to be … Danya.

TOBY. Maybe that's a girl I'd like to know. The one who keeps going for her friends.

(Beat. They are close now. **DANYA** *is actually calm.)*

DANYA. Honey ran off because she's angry with me. Maybe she should be. But we didn't know what to do after – the look in Honey's eyes when they buried her sister. Then at Ellen's wake… for hours everyone's eyes lifeless, eating cheese and crackers, pasting on smiles, like they're dead themselves. Honey, silent on the couch watching the videos we'd made – I can't watch them any more – but Honey is glued to them and then it plays – that last day in the park and Honey starts crying. I grab her, tell her we need to – we turn it off. *(beat)* We came here like we planned. "For Samagashi!" For Ellen, but now… I should never have brought Honey here. If only I knew where she was! I need to find her.

TOBY. Here we all know each other at a glance. Looking at a costume. But you know Honey –

DANYA. Better than anyone. If I give myself the time to feel what she's – feeling! If we imagine –

TOBY. – we can see her! Together. Where she would go.

*(***TOBY*** *and* ***DANYA*** *grasp hands and face out.)*

DANYA. Honey – where are you are?

(Fantasy music. They close their eyes and the projected settings around them begin to switch to different locations in the con – as she's "looking" for **HONEY.** *We hear the sounds of the convention – people arguing about comics, comparing costumes, telling stories, etc. Then she hears* **HONEY**'s *voice: "Almost there! Let me through please!" as she pushes through the crowd.* **DANYA** *sees her running.)*

DANYA. I see her! She's running. She's running to where she thinks she's safe! But she's in trouble. I have to get out of here!

(She snaps them out. Lights go back to normal. The sounds of reality, the elevator music creeps back in. The

others start moving again. The **GOTH PRINCESSES,**
and the other teens reform the elevator, crammed together,
and stuck.)

GOTH GIRL PRINCESS. We're going to be stuck here forever!

DANYA. No!

(**DANYA** *pulls the heavy elevator doors open! She runs*
out!)

GOTH GIRL PRINCESS. She has the power of the true geek!

GOTH BOY PRINCESS. GO GIRL!

TOBY. *(calling after* **DANYA***)* You're welcome!

Scene 2: Take What You Want

(HONEY is in SQUEAKER's Corner, surrounded by candy and oversized, brightly colored decorations.)

HONEY. Squeaker's Candy Corner! Just me alone. Well good! Good! I wanted to be alone. Who cares about seeing Samagashi or Danya. *(She's not having fun.)* This is so freakin' fun!

(She hears someone giggle behind her.)

Danya –?

(DEVIL CATS enter.)

DEVIL CAT ONE. Ah. Very nice. Purrrr. The little one –

DEVIL CAT TWO. All alone with –

DEVIL CAT ONE. A gift!

(They push her down and rip the bag from her hands.)

HONEY. Hey! Stop!

DEVIL CAT #1. Sorry little one – you'll learn when you're older – you take what you want.

DEVIL CAT #2. You should see the stuff we have for Samagashi to sign. We're gonna make a mint selling it all!

HONEY. You can't take that – it's not for you. It's all I have!

DEVIL CAT #2. Aw. Should we give her a little parting gift to remember us by?

(The DEVIL CATS push HONEY to the ground! They raise their cosplay claws about to fight her. HONEY cries for help. Suddenly there's a rumbling followed by a Squeak! Squeak! Squeak! An adorable bright "Totoro" – PacMan – like creature appears. It's a kid cosplaying in this huge, round orange ball outfit with big eyes and expressive eyebrows. HONEY lights up as if she might burst with happiness. It's like when you see the character that meant the most to you as kid come to life in front of you! Well, that might not have happened to you but

imagine it here! The mysterious cosplayer roars at the
DEVIL CATS *who run off.)*

HONEY. Squeaker?

(He happily squeaks and nods his head yes!)

Squeaker! Wow what a costume.

(He jumps up and down! He loves compliments.)

Okay! Whoever you are in there, I need your help.
Those awful cat women took – something very important. Means the world to me – we can't let them get
away, ok? Hmmm, you can't fly like in the cartoon but
– you can run very fast?

*(***SQUEAKER*** squeaks yes!)*

Let's get 'em! Virgie. Squeaker! Gooo!

(Anime music up! **HONEY** *and* **SQUEAKER** *pursue the*
DEVIL CATS *exiting after them. On the other side of the*
stage, The **DEVIL CATS** *enter, proud of themselves for*
scoring the bag. **HONEY** *enters and throws a huge ball*
of yarn at them. They drop the bag and \she grabs it!
SQUEAKER *runs in and sticks out his green tongue [an*
arm] which holds a spray bottle. He sprays. They hiss
and run away. **HONEY** *and* **SQUEAKER** *win!* **HONEY**
holds the bag high in the air and she goes to high five
SQUEAKER *but he makes a mad face. He has no arms!*
Lights out on **SQUEAKER** *and* **HONEY**.*)*

(Light up on **DANYA** *who enters, running. She stops,*
looking around confused.)

DANYA. Where am I?

MANNO. You are here.

DANYA. What? Who are you?

MANNO. Beware how you enter and who you trust in the
game room. I mean the Swamps of Malebolge!

DANYA. Only the Sorcerer Manno talks like that.

MANNO. It's true.

DANYA. *(slowly)* Are you Manno?

MANNO. Yes, I am.

*(A **KID** dressed as a wizard reveals himself proudly. He holds a big binder book. The cover is happily and colorfully decorated.)*

DANYA. It's me Dante – let me in!

MANNO. Manno would like to know if you have your flaming sword.

DANYA. Yes!

MANNO. Prove it to Manno!

DANYA. Right!

*(**DANYA** pushes a button on her sword. It lights up.)*

MANNO. Ah! You really are Dante! You are here!

DANYA. Yes, and oh god, I hate these words, but time is short. Can you –

MANNO. *(eagerly)* Yes?

DANYA. – help me?

MANNO. I don't understand these contemporary words.

DANYA. All right. *(acting like* **DANTE***)* I am seeking hospitality, oh great wizard. I'm looking for Squeaker's Candy Corner –

MANNO. It's right through the gaming room.

DANYA. Great! So, I can just –

MANNO. Manno doesn't want Dante to leave Malebolge! Manno commands Dante to stay.

DANYA. Command this, wacko!

MANNO. Manno Dante trap go!

(A trap falls on her.)

DANYA. Ah!

*(**DANYA** is dragged further into the darkness.)*

Scene 3: Spirits of the Undead

(Video projection #5: ELLEN, DANYA *and* HONEY *are dressed up as their characters. They are cosplaying during the day in a park.)*

ELLEN. *(as* CLEO*)* Just give it up Dante! Your home planet is doomed!

DANYA. *(as* DANTE*)* Never Cleo! I'll take care of you faster than your demon dogs at the porthole of Hell!

ELLEN. *(as* CLEO*)* At the price of your trusty guide?

*(*ELLEN *reveals* HONEY. HONEY *pretends she is tied up and hanging.)*

HONEY. *(as* VIRGIE*)* Dante help!

DANYA. *(as* DANTE*)* Virgie! Cleo! Suspending your own sister over the death river of boiling blood and fire? Why are you doing this? What's wrong with you?

ELLEN. *(personal, breaking character)* What's wrong with you, Danya?

DANYA. Character names.

ELLEN. Get off my case, D!

DANYA. If you're mad at me Ellen just say it!

ELLEN. These videos are for us to show Samagashi. But you just want to show off. You post them – online!

DANYA. Only on the DF chat room! Ellen. You're so worried about Honey, but when do you ever stand up to anybody.

ELLEN. You're one to talk!

*(*ELLEN *has taken the camera off its tripod. She follows* DANYA *filming/confronting her.* DANYA*'s responses are directly to the camera/*ELLEN*.)*

You're always on our case, but you're the one who hides in the hall. You're the one who's always running away.

DANYA. I don't care about anyone else. You guys are all I care about.

ELLEN. *(off camera)* And do you know what kind of pressure that is? You always want it to be me and you against the world, but what if I wasn't here?

DANYA. *(serious)* What does that mean? Ellen?

(video ends)

(Darkness. Tick! Tick! Tick! Time is almost running out now! Lights of harsh reality snap up as **DANYA** *wakes up to discover* **MANNO** *has tied her up.)*

MANNO. *(singing)* Manno brings you, Dante! Manno is fantastic! Manno rules the world! Through magic! Ho. Ho. Behold!

DANYA. Let me go! This isn't sorcery – this is kidnapedry!

MANNO. Oh, I like that!

DANYA. The con is about to close. I have to find my friend – we have to see Samagashi.

MANNO. Duh, I know.

DANYA. How?

MANNO. Mind reading card. And you're all over Miss Cosy's newscam. "Wanted."

DANYA. You're turning me in?

MANNO. Yes! Turning you into awesome! Behold *Dante's Fire* the Gathering Super Magic War Card Game Party!

(Christmas lights flick on in an awful room that smells bad with just a guy, cosplaying as a **TROLL** *with an ax planted in his head, in a lonely corner flipping cards.)*

Yes! A magical party of war – it says so right here in the guide: 6:40 *Dante's Fire* the Gathering Super Magic War Card Game Party! – and – we're so lonely. War makes it so. The ENEMY.

DANYA. The enemy?

MANNO. The stupid *Dante's Fire* "Elven Society" who got the main gaming room. Listen! Listen – to the mockery of – the Enemy!

*(***MANNO*** *opens a door. We hear amazing DJ music and laughter. We see the colorful lights flashing and confetti*

blows in from the happy room. The **TROLL** *decides it's a much better party and leaves, despite* **MANNO**'s *protests, slamming the door.)*

Damn. Another soldier lost in battle. This War of Magic ends today! Manno has you, Dante. And Manno, I, he, will win!

(Sprong! An arrow lands right next to **MANNO** *just missing him!* **SPRING** *rushes in, her bow is aimed and ready.)*

SPRING. Give it up, Manno! Dante is ours! And our elven glorious Larping parties of Malebolge will last for all time!

MANNO. No!

SPRING. Yes!

DANYA. No!

(A **KID** *dressed as a dwarf rushes in.)*

TINY AJAX. No!

MANNO & SPRING. TINY AJAX!

TINY AJAX. Tiny Ajax claims Dante! Malebolge will be ours for glorious roleplaying!

MANNO. Oh, give it up, Josh – dice? Manno will win because he holds the card of truth!

DANYA. Truth? Truth? You want the truth? You're all fighting about something that means nothing! You! You probably made your elven bow and arrow with your own hands. From a tree you widdled. And I bet you wore it in your school play of the hobbit or something.

SPRING. They put me in the back row. Amateurs!

DANYA. And you want to role play with some sexy cheerleader, but most likely you end up rolling with some cosplay chic. And there's nothing wrong with that!

TINY AJAX. Her name is Minnie. She's a minotaur.

DANYA. Whatever! And you, Manno! True to form. You say you're a magician and believe in magic, but you're just fighting with Spring because you want her to date you and vice versa!

MANNO. Our love can never be – she's an elf!

SPRING. Racist! *(She crosses her arms defiantly.)*

TINY AJAX. *(about* **DANYA***)* She has the magic! She is a prophet of the future!

DANYA. No. I know this because I dress up like Dante to try to play the hero when in real life, I screw up all the time. I'm supposed to see Samagashi. It's the last thing I promised a friend. And I failed her even though she's not here. Ellen's not coming back. She's never coming back! And the one friend I have living, I pissed off so badly that she ran off, and now she's in real trouble. I have to do something. I have to save, Honey. Please!

*(Heroic music swells. **DANYA** breaks free of her chains! It's awesome! They all bow down.)*

SPRING. It is you. The Dante in the videos. Three girls. You, Honey, Ellen. What happened to your friend affects us all. If anyone deserves to see Samagashi, it's you.

TINY AJAX. We are so sorry.

MANNO. This war of magic! It's torn us apart.

SPRING. Well it was never really a war –

MANNO. This stupid war. Can we amend?

*(They nod yes, getting emotional. They rise and raise their hands to **DANYA**. They then start singing a song of peace or dancing to blaring Irish folk music around her. It's insane. **DANYA** breaks the circle to leave.)*

DANYA. Can you crazy woodland kids just stop? Please.

*(**SPRING** reaches out and grabs **DANYA**'s arm – she has a "vision." Fantasy lighting. **SPRING**'s voice becomes other worldly.)*

SPRING. You seek Samagashi, but you have lost the very reason you have come here.

MANNO. She speaks the truth – it says so on the truth card!

SPRING. You seek the spirits of the undead.

DANYA. Yes.

SPRING. Go to Honey. She needs you. You must hurry. There is only one way to save her and to continue your quest to Samagashi.

(*Ominous music or sound.* **SPRING** *points to the other door that we didn't notice before. It gleams red.*)

TINY AJAX. We can't send her in there.

SPRING. It is the only way.

DANYA. Why? What's in there?

SPRING. Only what you fear. Only one road. To find the one who is living and the one who is dead.

DANYA. This is crazy.

SPRING. Welcome to Crazy Town, Dante-Danya. We all have to be little mad to even be here, oui?

(**SPRING** *gives* **DANYA** *her canteen.*)

Drink this.

DANYA. What is it? Some "magical drink?"

SPRING. A little of this and that.

MANNO. I love it when your dad is away and leaves his liquor cabinet unlocked.

SPRING. Yes, it is magical.

(**DANYA** *drinks.*)

No one faces the spirits of the undead sober.

DANYA. Ohhhhhh.

(**DANYA** *goes to door. It opens. A strong wind blows.*)

It's cold.

SPRING. It always is before you reach Hell.

(**DANYA** *exits. Lighting returns to normal.* **MANNO** *and* **TINY AJAX** *turn to* **SPRING**.)

MANNO. You really saw all that in your vision.

SPRING. It's what she needed to hear.

TINY AJAX. I hope she makes it.

SPRING. So hope we all.

Scene 4: Choice

(**HONEY** *and* **SQUEAKER** *are celebrating their victory, jumping up and down.*)

HONEY. We got my bag back – yes! Oh man whoever you are – you are the best!

(**SQUEAKER** *squeaks and excitedly points to her as if to say, "No you are the best!"*)

You're right! When I am Virgie, I am the best! I am! A trusty right-hand gal and guide who always knows everything and where she's going. So confident and cool!

(**SQUEAKER** *squeaks in agreement.*)

Right? Right! *(clutches bag)* Well, thanks again. I bet you have to go. This place closes in like twenty minutes – I can't imagine you want to spend your last few minutes with a stranger.

(*He squeaks sadly and starts to go.*)

Most people think your character, Squeaker, was put in the *Dante's Fire* TV show to use for exposition so my character Virgie could spill her guts when everything went wrong. And man, why is everything going so wrong? We got what we wanted and I could totally make it to Samagashi now on my own. I know I can now, but – oh! I don't know what to do. I know this isn't your problem but – You aren't going to take your costume off are you.

(*He shakes head "no."*)

You're going to keep playing –

(*He nods his head "yes."*)

Because you obviously spent a lot of time on that costume! You've even got some spy-looking, super faraway hearing device in there – because that's Squeaker's skill!

(**SQUEAKER** *is excited she notices. He nuzzles her.*)

Okay, Squeaker? I've been pretty mad lately. Really mad. And now I've got what we made –

(HONEY *opens the bag and shows what's inside: a lovingly decorated DVD case.*)

We put together all the videos – what my sister, Danya, and I – we've been working on them for so long. It's all our own – all the moments with all the Samagashi characters we love. It's what we wanted to show Samagashi – that was the plan until… It's really messed up, and I don't have anyone to talk to …! I just need someone to listen. My sister and I we came home from the park after the worst day we'd ever had. I was crying… she… She didn't cry. She took off her Cleo armor. Her jacket. She sat there in her jeans and t-shirt in front of the mirror. "Leave me alone, Honey," she said. I was mad that she wouldn't talk to me. I slammed the door. That was the last time I saw her… A week ago my sister died. It was her choice. And we chose to come here like it's some kind of quest, like if we meet Samagashi – like that would change anything?

(HONEY *shoves the bag with the DVD away. It slides across the room.* SQUEAKER *squeaks and pushes it back towards* HONEY. *He nuzzles her.* HONEY *picks it up. Realizing.*)

But whatever choice I make now – is my choice.

SQUEAKER. Squeak!

HONEY. And I'm not anything like Virgie, but it is – it's making me who I want to be! And who cares if I get laughed at for liking the coolest kid in school?

(SQUEAKER *nods.*)

Like that's going to work out – being in love with Bobby Branden.

(SQUEAKER *expresses interest in this.*)

I know there's no way the cutest guy in school would ever be into me but –

(**SQUEAKER** *kisses her or licks her with his tongue.*)

Well, I know you love me, Squeaker. I raised you from an egg on the planet of Glock!

SQUEAKER. *(alarmed)* Squeak! Squeak!

HONEY. What's wrong?

SQUEAKER. SQUEAK! SQUEAK!

HONEY. Your super hearing device! You heard something! Danya's in trouble? She's calling for me? She needs me? Oh! I have to choose now. Not what Virgie would do but me. We have to help her! Let's go!

(**SQUEAKER** *and* **HONEY** *race off.*)

Scene 5: The End of Dante

(**DANYA** *enters – she's high up now – in an unfinished room. It has a huge back wall – that reflects back on her – a hall of mirrors. She is unsteady – clearly* **SPRING**'s *drink has had an effect on her.*)

DANYA. Honey? Honey! Can you hear me?

(*Lights shift. Video projection #6:* **DANYA** *sees images of herself,* **HONEY**…*and* **ELLEN***. The last video they shot. Time wise this video is later in the day from video #4, picking up from where it left off, with the girls cosplaying in the park.* **DANYA** *is confronted by this projection, which fills the back wall. She backs away. This day is her greatest fear. She falls to the floor. She'd love to turn away, but she can't stop watching the dialogue/action in the video.*)

ELLEN. (*as* **CLEO**) So this is it! The end of Dante.

DANYA. (*as* **DANTE**) Stop! I don't want to hurt you.

ELLEN. (*as* **CLEO**) But I want to hurt YOU!

HONEY. (*as* **VIRGIE**) Sister! We just want to help you! We want you to be happy!

ELLEN. (*as* **CLEO**) You have no idea what makes me happy! You never have.

DANYA. (*as* **DANTE**) But we've come all this way to bring you … home.

ELLEN. (*as* **CLEO**) Sweet, Sweet Dante – No one – no FREAKING one – can bring home the dead. Poor, poor, Dante.

(*The sound of* **PUNKS** *laughter. The girls are not alone in the park. All immediately drop character. They look to each other, scared.*)

Danya –

(*The* **PUNKS** *have the camera. They lift it up off the tripod. The following is filmed from their perspective as they film* **ELLEN, DANYA** *and* **HONEY** *running away* *from them. Mocking them as they run. The horrible things they say overlap:)*

PUNK #1. You want to play pretend? What the hell are you lame freaks supposed to be – Losers. Crazy looking weirdos – That's right! Go! Look at them run! Look at them RUN like little babies.

(DANYA stops running away. She starts to turn back.)

ELLEN. Danya! What are you doing?

(DANYA faces them.)

PUNKS. Oh…you want some more, huh?

(As they speak the below, DANYA is walking towards them, and in effect the camera. Her walk gets stronger as their words reach a crescendo.)

Idiot. Loser. Moron. Skank. Ho. Lame-ass-GEEK!

(She is directly in front of the camera now. ELLEN and HONEY run to DANYA, joining her by her side. They are face to face with the PUNKS, all three side by side. DANYA raises her sword.)

DANYA. I'm not afraid of you!

(PUNKS descend upon them. We hear the sounds of fighting and DANYA, HONEY and ELLEN yelling back at them, their voices blending together, "Get away", "Stop", "I hate you". The camera is tossed like a ball, like a horror movie. The projection goes out.)

(DANYA, on stage, is in a corner shivering, crying.)

DANYA. Ellen.

(A masked CLEO FIGURE appears projected – or as an actor stalking DANYA in the space.)

Who's there? *(DANYA quickly turns and sees.)* Cleo? Who are you? Tell me who you are!

CLEO FIGURE. Why? You never listen.

DANYA. Stop acting like…

CLEO FIGURE. I am who you think I am, Dante.

DANYA. I'm going crazy. You're crazy. I'm not going to fight you.

CLEO FIGURE. Dante running away? Again?

DANYA. I've got to find Honey.

CLEO FIGURE. Character names. You mean Virgie, don't you?

DANYA. Who are you?

CLEO FIGURE. I know who I am. You're the one who's so unsure of herself she lashes out at everyone. Isn't that right? Because she looks in the mirror and what does she see…? A small pathetic little girl.

DANYA. Shut up! I'm not cosplaying a stranger.

CLEO FIGURE. Who says I'm a stranger. Virgie? She's gone. She's already seen Samagashi.

DANYA. No way. She wouldn't.

CLEO FIGURE. And then she left. Left you here all alone. Just like everyone leaves. Poor, poor, Dante. Alone.

DANYA. SHUT UP! I don't need anything. I don't need anyone. And I sure don't need YOU!

(**DANYA** goes after the figure but the figure reacts – a live masked actor appears – has **DANYA** by the throat!)

CLEO FIGURE. The spirits of the undead demand vengeance!

(This masked **CLEO** pushes **DANYA** to the ground. **HONEY** rushes in, the bag slung across her shoulders.)

DANYA. Honey – you came back!

(**SQUEAKER** rushes in.)

SQUEAKER. SQUEAKKK!

DANYA. Squeaker?

HONEY. You're lucky I did come back. Who is this … Danya? Who is she?

(**SQUEAKER** leaps towards the masked **CLEO**.)

CLEO FIGURE. You think the Spirits of Undead can be defeated by some pet?

HONEY. Hey! Don't make him mad. He'll eat your face.

(*HONEY pushes her into* **SQUEAKER***'s mouth. The masked* **CLEO FIGURE** *struggles. Speaker lets go and she stumbles, facing full front – her mask has been ripped off by* **SQUEAKER**.)

DANYA & HONEY. Gwen!

(**GWEN** *grabs the bag back from* **HONEY**. *She runs to the ledge, holding the bag out over it.*)

GWEN. I shouldn't have made fun of you guys, but what do you expect? You come here and drive us all crazy like you're better than everyone. You give me a bloody nose for what – for this, this bag?

DANYA. Stop!

HONEY. Just give it back.

GWEN. You want this so bad. It means that much to you?

DANYA. Yes, Gwen. It means everything. Now, hand it over.

GWEN. Get away from me! Woah!

(**GWEN** *starts to fall.*)

Ahhh! Danya!

(**DANYA** *grabs* **GWEN**. **HONEY** *grabs* **DANYA** *and reaches out to* **SQUEAKER** *who grabs her arm in his mouth.*)

Danya, help!

DANYA. Gwen! Hold on.

GWEN. I can't. I'm slipping!

(**GWEN** *slips. Lights bump to black. In darkness we hear* **GWEN** *screaming! The following dialogue happens rapidly in darkness.*)

HONEY. Danya what are you doing?

DANYA. Honey, trust me. C'mon. Jump!

(*sound of wind racing past* **DANYA** *and* **HONEY**…)

DANYA & HONEY. AHHH!!!

DANYA. (*while falling, her voice getting further away*) For Samagashi .....

(THUMP! Sound of landing on something. The fantasy lights bump up on the girls clinging to **SQUEAKER** *who now has huge wings. Flying fantasy music plays as they "soar!")*

DANYA. Oh, my god!

HONEY. Look down!

GWEN. Or don't…! Yikes!

DANYA. We're gliding!

GWEN. We're flying!

HONEY. Yes! Squeaker, you're amazing! You saved us, whoever you are! You really did it!

SQUEAKER. Squeak! Squeak!

DANYA. We're gonna make it! Samagashi, we're coming!

Scene 6: Power Of The Stars

(DANYA, HONEY *and* GWEN *"drop" into a room.*
SQUEAKER *"flies" away.*)

SQUEAKER. SQUEAK!

HONEY. He's gliding on! Goodbye friend … whoever you
are.

(GWEN *gives* DANYA *back the bag.* DANYA *slings it
across her shoulders.*)

DANYA. *(to* GWEN*)* Come with us. The guest artist suite and
Samagashi are right through that door!

GWEN. But there are guards! *(stepping back, scared)* We'll
never get past them.

DANYA. There's always a way! You just imagine and whatever
you want can happen. That's how we play. *(realizing –
turning to* HONEY*)* That's how we've always played.

HONEY. We can show you. Right, Danya? Because acting
out stories in your backyard or here – they aren't just
stories – it's real and they mean something. And when
you make it real and you have friends to count on, you
can fight anything that comes your way. Because that's
what you need to keep going. Danya?

DANYA. *(truly confident)* You become a hero. We are Dante
and Virgie and Cleo – and those aren't just guards!

ALL. They're Devil Guards!

*(Fantasy lighting. Sound of heavy footsteps, crackling
the floor apart. The* GUARDS *appear again, but this
time they have devil horns and huge devil hands! They
block the girls from the artists' entrance. Red alert lights
come on. The animated* MISS COSY *appears projected.)*

MISS COSY. This area is off limits. Guest Artists Only. Oh,
it's you! The Con's Most Wanted: Dante, Virgie, and
Cleo! Bad Bad naughty-lings! Give up now! Stop where
you are!

DANYA. Nothing is stopping us from going through that door! C'mon!

MISS COSY. End friendly Miss Cosy application.

(Her eyes turn red! Multiple projected images of **MISS COSY** *fill the walls with her now evil, angry face! They all speak with an evil voice.)*

This is the end of Dante!

DANYA. I have another idea.

HONEY. Which is…?

DANYA. *Dante's Fire,* o' my darlings!

DANYA, HONEY, & GWEN. GO!

(Anime music up! The girls rush. The **DEVIL GUARD** *minions attack! They fight in exaggerated movements!* **DANYA** *is thrown back, recovering. She sees* **GWEN** *is getting hurt – and suddenly* **HONEY** *is in danger!)*

DANYA. Honey!

HONEY. Danya! What does Dante do?

*(***DANYA** *looks at the sword she holds.)*

DANYA. The power of the stars. The hope of the Universe.

*(***HONEY** *escapes from a* **GUARD**. *She runs to the sword, holding it with* **DANYA**.*)*

Sword of flame from which you were forged – make us one! Now!

(Intense, inspiring Fantasy J-Pop sounds and music. Suddenly bright lights swirl around them – the power of the stars! An explosion – the **GUARDS** *are blown away by the power, tumbling off stage. The three girls come together with their backs to the audience. They look up at the stars [projected], which appear in the sky.)*

GWEN. Go. Fight. Win! Yeah!

DANYA. Together! *(turning to* **HONEY***)* I will always be there for you, Honey. No one will ever hurt you as long as there is breath in me. I promise you that.

*(***HONEY** *takes* **DANYA***'s hand.)*

ANNOUNCER. *(matter-of-factly tone)* Congratulations *Dante's Fire* cosplayers for another great con. Dante's Fire Con is officially over. Thank you for coming.

(Harsh lights come back on, coming back to reality. The girls squint.)

GWEN. Uh, well…it's been…

DANYA. Gwen…thanks.

GWEN. *(wanting to say more, but gets awkward)* Whatever. Later!

(GWEN runs off. She passes GUARD #2 who enters ushering everyone out.)

GUARD #2. Okay. Nothing to see here. C'mon, it's over people. Move on out. Families. Lives. Phantom Menace on Spike TV, all these things await.

(GUARD #2 crosses stage and exits. SQUEAKER and TOBY enter, following along behind the guard unnoticed by him.)

HONEY. Squeaker, you're back! I'll miss you. Thank you for everything.

(She hugs SQUEAKER. Turns to go but SQUEAKER takes off his costume.)

Bobby Branden?!

BOBBY. Yeah, um, wow it's hot in there.

HONEY. Yes. Yes I can imagine it is.

DANYA. Toby…! *(DANYA rushes up. She hugs him, then retreats.)* Thank you.

TOBY. For what?

DANYA. Being Toby. I'd pick you over Ulee-o any day.

TOBY. Well, some days it's hard to tell us apart.

BOBBY. You're pretty great.

HONEY. Really?

BOBBY. And – we will most definitely keep in touch. Next week after school. My house.

HONEY. I'm totally there.

*(**BOBBY** grins and exits.)*

DANYA. I just wish… Ellen. I just wish she was…

TOBY. Here.

DANYA. Yeah.

TOBY. She is. "Two best friends play the best they ever have in her honor."

DANYA. That's sweet, but –

TOBY. No, I'm quoting. "For Ellen." It's already tweeted all over the chat room.

DANYA. Huh, I wonder who wrote that?

TOBY. Maybe a tall kick ass guy. I mean, I don't know, yo.

DANYA. *(grinning)* I bet, yo.

TOBY. So… Next year? Or, if you ever come to New York? Brooklyn. Call me.

DANYA. Don't count on it.

*(**TOBY** gives her a smile.)*

Maybe.

TOBY. *(tossing her his helmet)* To remember me by. Til then, o' my darling.

*(**TOBY** takes her hand and kisses it with a flourish. He exits. **DANYA** smiles, looking after him. **HONEY** is there watching her, smiling too. They turn to leave, running smack into **GUARD TWO** who peers down at them. Clearly recognizing them.)*

GUARD #2. Watch where you're going kid. There's a Dante and Virgie on the loose, and I'm supposed to bring 'em in…if I find them.

DANYA. Uh…yeah.

GUARD #2. But I don't see them around here. *(whispers, confiding)* You know, I used to be a member of the rebel alliance when I was a kid.

*(**DANYA** bows to **GUARD #2**. She holds out her Sword of Fire.)*

DANYA. For you good solider, wield it well.

(**GUARD #2** *takes the sword.* **HONEY** *and* **DANYA** *start to go.*)

GUARD #2. Hey, I wouldn't take that exit. It's a little too crowed. *(pointing out other exit)* That door – yeah – that's the one I'd take. Puts you out right by Parking Lot B.

DANYA. Why?

GUARD #2. Teenagers! So many questions! Just scat, will you?

(**HONEY** *and* **DANYA** *are the last to walk out. Slam of the doors. The whole convention is for the first time empty, peaceful.* **GUARD #1** *enters.*)

GUARD #1. Did you really think you could help your friends escape – Skywalker.

GUARD #2. Actually… You can call me Dante.

(**GUARD #2** *holds up the Sword of Fire. It lights up.* **GUARD #1** *reveals he has a* **STEAMPUNK** *Army hat. Puts it on.*)

GUARD #1. Ulee-o, yo.

(*Oh! The two* **GUARDS** *go at each other – making out passionately and crazy!*)

Scene 7: A Clear Way

(Harsh reality: **HONEY** *and* **DANYA** *enter the parking lot, finishing putting on the sweatshirts over their costumes they were wearing at the start of the play. They now look again like* **HONEY** *and* **DANYA**, *but there's a sense of something different about them.)*

HONEY. It's so cool out here. Danya...?

DANYA. I'll get the Chrysler.

*(***DANYA*** starts to go.)*

HONEY. Danya...it isn't...your fault. She made a choice.

(beat)

DANYA. I'll get the car.

(A **FIGURE** *appears walking towards them. Her back is towards us. But* **HONEY** *sees that she looks familiar...)*

HONEY. Danya. Is that – ?

(The **FIGURE** *walks past them, but* **DANYA** *calls out.)*

DANYA. Ms. Samagashi.

*(***SAMAGASHI*** stops and turns.)*

I don't know why you're stopping. I don't know why you're listening to me. But this morning – we buried our friend. Ellen. They put her in the ground between gravestones and no one will know where lies the best Cleo there ever was. She was my best friend. Her sister Honey and I – we'd make up stories and we just wanted to show you.

*(***DANYA*** hands her the bag. **SAMAGASHI** takes out the DVD they've made. She looks at its carefully decorated case, then looks back to* **DANYA**, *listening.)*

We wanted to give this to you because she loved you and your world and we loved being a part of it with her. Because it helped us feel – like we belonged. Somewhere. Because we don't know why she...we don't know why she chose to – and I don't know how to –

(SAMAGASHI *touches* DANYA's *arm.* SAMAGASHI *pulls* DANYA *close, whispers something in her ear. Then exits.* DANYA *looks after her.*)

HONEY. What did she say? Danya, what did she say?

DANYA. "Live long enough. Live long enough to be –"

HONEY. To be.

DANYA. "Live long enough to be old. And you will. You will understand 'o my darl –"

(DANYA *is crying.* HONEY *almost does too, but instead she takes* DANYA's *arm. She looks up at the sky.* DANYA *does too.*)

The stars. You can see them so clear. It's so clear.

HONEY. Yes. It is.

(GWEN, *in normal clothes, runs on.*)

GWEN. Guys! Hey, guys.

HONEY. Hey.

GWEN. I was just wondering... Turn out that Minnie The Minotaur said she'd give me a ride, but –

HONEY. She can't drive.

GWEN. Yeah. Her parents picked her up. I'm not too far away from you guys if that's not too ... ?

DANYA. C'mon, Gwen, Honey, let's go home.

(*Beat.* DANYA *takes out her iphone. She presses play.* Dante's Fire *theme plays.* DANYA *puts an arm around* HONEY, *then around* GWEN. *They look at each other. Smile. The stars of the universe shine around them. Growing brighter as they exit.*)

(*Immediate blackout.*)

End of Play

Extras: Danya Running Montage/Car Sequence

[Note: It's possible to show Danya's journey from rushing out of the Elevators leaving Toby, at the end of Act Two, Scene 1, before Act Two, Scene 2 where Honey, in Squeaker's Candy Corner, is attacked by the Devil Cats. It can be super fun, provides Danya her own montage through staging, video, or puppetry, and adds a wicked jolt to the storytelling. Enjoy!]

(Video projection #5: An Animated "Run Danya Run" video where **DANYA** *races through the con to reach* **HONEY***! It's also possible to do this with puppets or on-stage theatrically. The dialogue below is in the video/ can be used on stage.)*

DANYA. What the hell is with this crowd? No one's moving!

MISS COSY. All hail the winner of our Dante's Schoolgirls Naughty Milkshakes Trivia Game – winning this one of a kind Lifesize *Dante's Fire* 5000 Commando Car Mobile! Minnie the Minotaur! YAY!

MINNIE. YES!!! I win! I win! I never –

DANYA. Sorry but I have to commandeer this vehicle for very extreme cosplaying circumstances.

MINNIE. What? NOOO!!!

*(***DANYA** *jumps into the car!)*

DANYA. Oh god how does this – ?

DANTE'S FIRE MOBILE. Name your destination.

DANYA. FREAKING GPS! THANK YOU TONKA! Squeaker's Candy Corner and hurry!

DANTE'S FIRE MOBILE. Buckle up.

DANYA. Oh. No shit. Here we freaking –

DANTE FIRE MOBILE. GO!!!

DANYA. WOOO-HOOO!!!

*(***DANYA** *takes off faster than Batman! Video/scene ends.)*

[Note: If you stage the above, then add the following action to Act Two, Scene 3 right after the cosplaying video, and right before Danya meets Manno.]

*(Meanwhile, we hear **DANYA** racing through the con in her* Dante's Fire *Mobile. We hear people screaming for her to look where she's going! Crash! A tire wheel or bent steering wheel rolls on stage. **DANYA** enters holding her head, dazed. She takes in her surroundings. It looks like some kind of swampy battlefield, full or rubble.)*

DANYA. Where am I?

VOICE. Here.

[resume scene]

DANTE'S FIRE

Cosplay Character Illustrations

Dante

Illustration © Kristina Makowski

Dante

Illustration © Jessica Wegener Shayy

Virgie

Illustration © Kristina Makowski

Virgie

Illustration © Jessica Wegener Shay

Cleo

Illustration © Kristina Makowski

Cleo

Illustration © Jessica Wegener Shay

Ulee-o

Illustration © Kristina Makowski

Squeaker

Illustration © Kristina Makowski